TRICKS

(a *Take It Off* novel)

Love can play tricks on your heart…

After serving several years in the United States Marine Corps, Sergeant Tucker Patton decides to hang up his uniform and go to work at a private investigative firm owned by his buddy. His boxes are packed and he's got one foot out the door when a phone call changes everything.

Instead of going to North Carolina, he heads to New York City to literally step into the life of his twin brother, who died under suspicious circumstances. But pretending to be someone else isn't easy.

Especially when the person you're supposed to be is wanted dead.

Not only that, but he's going from being blissfully single to living with his brother's woman. An uptight, no-nonsense lawyer.

Charlotte Rose Carter doesn't have time for fun and games. She graduated with honors and made all the right moves fresh out of college to jumpstart her career as a successful young lawyer. She even snagged the most eligible bachelor in New York City's corporate world.

So what if her and Max's relationship isn't burning up the sheets? So what if their life doesn't read like a chapter from a sizzling romance novel? This is the real world, and in the real world that stuff is just fantasy.

Until it isn't.

Suddenly, just the slightest touch or a single glance from Max has her heart doing somersaults. Suddenly, the lackluster relationship begins to spark, and Charlotte finds herself tied in a knot of desire.

But she has no idea about the tricks being played right under her perky little nose.

"A new storyline that grabs you from page one and twists you into an action-packed ride full of danger and romance!"
—*USA Today* bestselling author Tabatha Vargo for *TEXT*

"Let me be clear—of the 1001 ways to die, burning would NOT be my first choice. However, a house consumed with flames and no chance of saving yourself equals RESCUE FANTASY FULFILLED."
—Scandalicious Book Reviews for *TORCH*

TRICKS

Take It Off Series

CAMBRIA HEBERT

Published by: Cambria Hebert Books, LLC

Cambria Hebert books, LLC.

your key to escape.

http://www.cambriahebert.com

Interior design and typesetting by Sharon Kay
Cover design by MAE I DESIGN
Edited by Cassie McCown
Copyright 2014 by Cambria Hebert
ISBN: 978-1-938857-40-9

Other books by Cambria Hebert

Heven and Hell Series

Before
Masquerade
Between
Charade
Bewitched
Tirade
Beneath
Renegade
Heven & Hell Anthology

Death Escorts

Recalled
Charmed

Take It Off

Torch
Tease
Tempt
Text
Tipsy

DEDICATION

For Sada Walker Maciel.

For being a reader. For being a friend.

The world needs more people like you.

You asked for a rocker… Well, Tucker has a guitar.

TRICKS

PROLOGUE

Max

The elevator doors dinged and slid open with barely a sound. Harsh yellow lighting shone down from the concrete ceiling and cast everything with a dirty glow as I stepped out into the underground parking garage. It was late, but that wasn't anything new. I worked late every night.

Most of the parking spots had been vacated hours ago, people going home to their families or to the gym to blow off steam. I didn't have time to blow off steam. I was too busy building a career.

And then the FBI showed up at my door.

They threatened my career. They threatened my reputation. My name.

I had no choice but to do what they asked.

The sound of a low scuffle from behind caused me to glance over my shoulder as I walked. No one was there, but that didn't stop my hackles from rising. I'd become paranoid these last few months. Yet it seemed paranoid people were that way for a reason.

I quickened my steps and fished the keys to my black Lincoln MKZ out of my pocket. They slid out of my fingers and made a clattering sound on the cold pavement. I bent to retrieve them, noticing the movement of a shadow beneath a car several rows away.

I knew then my paranoia wasn't just in my head.

Scooping up the keys, I closed the distance to my car and slid behind the wheel, throwing my briefcase into the back. Just before I started the engine I heard another engine roar to life.

My heart jumped up into my throat and pounded uncomfortably as I fired up the car and pulled quickly out of the parking spot. Because of the size and shape of the garage, speeding like I wanted to was almost impossible. As I rounded the corner into the next aisle of cars, my foot hovered anxiously over the gas pedal.

A dark four-door sedan pulled out behind me. I glanced into my rearview mirror, noting the ominous glow of the vehicle's parking lights.

I didn't speed up because I didn't want to give any indication that I knew that car back there was a threat to me. The longer I could play it cool, the better off I would be.

Focusing on the next turn, I steered the MKZ around the corner, noting the way the lights in the aisle flickered like some bad horror movie. I was certain if I rolled down my window I would hear the buzzing of the bad electrical connection that barely kept the lights lit.

A sudden squeal and the jolting of my car had me glancing around, out the back window.

"Shit," I yelled, unable to keep in the nervous energy swirling around inside me. The vehicle rammed into the back of me once again, jerking my car forward and causing it to fishtail slightly. I gripped the wheel tightly and fought for control as the passenger side of the MKZ narrowly missed a large concrete partition.

Screw driving like a granny.

My foot pounded down on the gas pedal and the engine responded immediately. The car shot forward as I spun the wheel, taking yet another curve. Shit! How far up did I have to go to get to street level? It didn't seem like it took this long to get down here.

'Course, I wasn't being chased then.

The Lincoln handled well, but the speed and force of the curve caused the back end to slam into one of the cars parked nearby. The sound of crunching metal and shattering glass filled the air and I gritted my teeth together and hit the gas again.

My car skidded forward and the entrance onto the street came into view. Holding the wheel steady, I focused on getting out into the street.

The black sedan behind rammed me again and a loud curse ripped from my throat. I had known the chances of getting caught were high, but I never thought they would come at me like this.

The sound of a revving engine had me glancing in the rearview mirror, again noting how dangerously close the car was to hitting me.

My foot held the gas pedal all the way against the floor as I smashed through the little gate where I was supposed to stop and slip a ticket into the machine. I didn't have time for that shit.

The sound of groaning metal and splitting wood followed me as the black car flew out of the mouth of the garage and into oncoming traffic. Drivers around me laid on their horns, blaring their anger as I landed in the center of the street, the MKZ paying no attention to the yellow lines dividing the pavement.

The sound of metal crunching against metal made me wince, but I didn't stop to survey the damage I caused. Instead, I kept driving. Smoke lingered in the air from the burn of my tires as I tore down the road. The few people on the sidewalks stopped to stare and the lit streetlights cast shadows behind them, making all the buildings look dark and ominous.

A quick check in the rearview mirror told me I was still being pursued. I loosened the tie around my neck and took a deep breath, still not easing up on the gas. Sweat was sliding down my back and gathering in my armpits and my heart was beating so rapidly it felt like it could explode at any moment.

The traffic light at an intersection just ahead turned red, signaling that it was time to stop. But I couldn't stop. Instead, I barreled through the four-way, narrowly missing a few cars and nearly losing control of the steering wheel.

My palms were sweaty. My grip was too loose.

"Fuck!" I roared when the car behind me did not let up.

I took a turn too sharply and the back end flipped around, my ride literally going sideways in the center of a street. *Where the hell are the cops? Shouldn't I at least hear sirens by now?* I was driving like a damn maniac.

Inside the pocket of my jacket was my cell and I dug it out and hit a button.

"Yes?" The voice came on the line.

"They know," I said, straightening out the vehicle and rushing down the street.

"Where are you?" he asked, calm.

"In my car. They're tailing me. I'm pretty sure they don't want to chat."

As if to punctuate my words, my car was rammed again. The force of the hit sent me jerking forward as my seatbelt tightened so tautly it was painful against my chest. All the air whooshed out of my body and I gasped for more.

"Where's the proof?"

"Somewhere safe."

"Where!" the voice demanded.

A deadly calm settled over me. It was fear. It was the truth. It was my future. I might be talking to the good guy right now… but even the good guys sometimes bent the rules. If I told him where the item he wanted was, he would leave me to die. He would consider me nothing more than collateral damage.

"Send help. Then I'll show you where it is myself," I said, my voice sounding strange to my own ears. In the midst of so much chaos, so much adrenaline rushing through my veins, I sounded almost bored.

"Where are you?" he asked, and I could hear papers being shuffled around and the movement of chairs in the background.

I gave him my location and the direction in which I was heading. "You better get here fast."

"We're on the way," he said tersely.

The momentary relief I felt caused me to lose focus and I drove up over the curb, hitting a brown, wooden electric pole that seemed to come out of nowhere. The impact was shocking, causing me to fly forward and smack my head on the steering wheel. The momentum flung me back into my seat, and I blinked through tearing eyes at my now motionless car.

The airbags hadn't deployed. That was a good thing, right? It meant the car wasn't so bad off I couldn't keep driving.

Trying to shake off the headache and nausea that was hitting me hard, I glanced out the windshield at the front side of my car. It was caved in. A busted mess. One of the headlights shattered and no longer worked and the engine was making an odd sort of wheezing sound.

"Max," the man said through the phone, which had fallen into the passenger seat upon impact.

I scooped up the phone and held it to my ear. "I'm still here."

"Tell me where it is," he urged, desperation tingeing his tone.

I rolled my head to the side, looking out the window, and saw it. The black sedan sat idling not far away. The windows were so darkly tinted that seeing inside was impossible. But it didn't matter who it was.

I knew who wanted me dead.

The passenger-side door opened and one black dress shoe stepped out, followed by the rest of a body of a man wearing a black suit. There was a gun in his hand.

Seeing that gun seemed to snap me back into reality and I jerked up, throwing the car into reverse. Sitting here was like inviting death.

"Max!" the man on the other line demanded.

I knew then I had to tell him. I couldn't use my life as a bargaining chip for the truth. I knew this was dangerous when I signed on. I knew that this had been a possibility.

I never thought I'd fail.

I reversed quickly, the car dropping off the sidewalk with a bang. I threw the gear into drive and started to speed away just as the man and his gun reached me. A bullet tore through the back window, shattering the glass.

"Max! Goddamn it! Tell me!"

"It's on its way."

"What the hell does that mean?" he roared.

The bullets kept on coming, one of them puncturing the back tire. The entire vehicle sagged unevenly as the tire groaned and made a loud rudding sound. I wasn't going to stop. I couldn't.

I drove down the street, the rim sparking against the pavement, making it look like I was throwing some kind of firework out the back window.

"Help is on the way, Max," the man promised, and I believed him. But I no longer thought they'd get here in time. "Please tell me where it is."

I opened my mouth to tell him. To tell him exactly what he wanted to know.

But the words never got free.

The black sedan came out of nowhere, barreling into the back of my car, sending me into a tailspin across the pavement. I spun in great circles, like the car was on a pair of ice skates and this was some kind of show. And then I slammed into a fire hydrant.

The MKZ flipped and began to roll through the street, all the windows shattered, glass raining every which way. The phone flew out of my hand and my eyes no longer saw.

It's true what they say.

Your life really does flash before your eyes right before you die.

Memories of being young, being carefree, flooded my head. I no longer felt the injuries that were hammering my body. I no longer felt the glass cutting into my skin or the tug and pull of a too-tight seatbelt.

I saw my first pet, my parents, my old baseball coach.

And then the car stopped flipping. It landed in a heap somewhere in the street. By then I heard sirens somewhere in the distance.

The screeching of tires had me blinking, blinking past the wet stickiness that was in my eyes. The men were still here, waiting to see if I would climb out of this wreck, waiting to see if they had to finish the job.

A face exactly like mine flashed into my thoughts. But it wasn't me I was seeing. It was my brother. My twin. So alike yet so different.

I couldn't die for nothing. I couldn't let them get away with what they'd done.

I coughed, testing out my voice. "Get Tucker," I said, my voice a mere whisper. That wasn't good enough.

"Get Tucker!" I said, projecting the two words as far as I could. Pain lanced through my insides. Everything hurt... It hurt so much.

If that phone was still somewhere inside this car, if it was still working, then they heard me. They would know what to do.

If there was anyone who could finish this job, it was Tucker.

Suddenly, I regretted all the hours I spent working. All the time I let slip right by. When was the last time I'd seen my brother? A year? Two?

Even still, I knew he would come.

I just wouldn't be here when he did.

The sharp smell of gasoline broke through my haze of pain and memories, and I started to struggle, to try and get myself free. I managed to get free of the seatbelt, and my body dropped into a heap onto the hood of the car. The driver's side window was busted out and I reached for the opening, ready to give all my strength to pulling myself through.

When my head cleared the window, I blinked through the night, looking around for the guy with the gun. No one was there. Not even the dark sedan. They were on the other side of the wreckage. They didn't see me trying to get free.

The sound of the sirens grew insistent and loud, and I breathed a sigh of relief as I knew they were very close by. Perhaps those hadn't been my last minutes. Perhaps I really would get out of this.

Hope was like balm to my tattered body. I felt my dry, cracked lips break into a smile.

These assholes were going down. And I was getting a second chance. A second chance at life. I wasn't going to work it away this time. This time I was going to live.

My torso cleared the wreckage and I stopped to gasp for breath.

A sudden burst of heat caught me off guard. Bright yellow and orange exploded into my vision. Before I could register any blistering pain, the explosion completely melted my body and turned it into ash.

There would be no second chance for me after all.

1

Tucker

My mouth felt like it was packed with cotton. You know that dry but slightly sticky feeling? My tongue moved and it brushed against the roof of my mouth and the cotton came with it.

I grunted and opened my eyes only to immediately shut them again. I wasn't ready for morning. *Shit, how much did I drink last night?* My body was still heavy with sleep, my limbs not wanting to get up and cooperate.

One of my arms was flung wide and I pulled it in to rub a hand over my sleepy face, hoping it would wake me up a little more. I knew I needed to get up… I just couldn't think of what the reason was.

Something shifted beside me and I felt the covers lift and drop. The soft sound of footsteps reached my ears. It wasn't a something. It was a *someone.*

I went home with someone last night.

Opening my eyes again, I glanced to my left in time to see a woman wearing nothing but a pink thong step into the adjoining bathroom and quietly close the door. Well, now I remembered the reason I went home with her.

Her ass was luscious.

Vague flashes of last night filtered through my hazy beer-soaked memory of skin against skin and a low, seductive laugh. What was her name again? Veronica? Violet? Shit, I hadn't a clue.

Tossing away the covers, I swung my legs over the side of the mattress and looked down. I was buck-ass naked. I looked around for my clothes, which were lying in a pile near the door of the bedroom.

Must have been in a hurry to get naked. I smirked. I was always in a hurry to get naked. Especially when I was with a woman with an ass like that.

I glanced back at the closed bathroom door as the toilet flushed and the tap water turned on. That was my cue to leave. I had my boxers and jeans on when the door opened.

Rushing out the door with shirt in hand seemed a little immature, so I turned. And, man, did I get an eyeful. There was no way in hell her boobs were real. They were too perfect. Large, round, creamy globes sat high atop her chest. They gave way to a flat stomach with a light-reflecting stud in her bellybutton. The pink thong was still in place but left little to the imagination and her long, tan legs stretched all the way to the floor.

Her hair was dark, her features exotic and her lips were full.

Even drunk, I had good taste.

I motioned with my chin, a little "what's up" gesture, and draped my T-shirt over my shoulder.

"Leaving so soon?" she asked, padding across the carpet toward me.

I didn't even pretend to not look at her chest. Shit, this had been a one-night stand. She could think I was a dog all she wanted. Hell, she'd be right.

'Course, she clearly wasn't the type of girl to be offended by my wandering eyes. She walked right up to me, wound her arms around my bare waist, and pressed those perfect tits right up against my chest. Then she rubbed around like she was a cat and I was her scratching pole.

"Don't you want to stay for breakfast?" she purred.

"Much as I'd like to, I can't. Got somewhere to be."

The woman, whose name might or might not be Veronica, pulled back and sashayed her ass across the room to a wooden nightstand by the bed. She bent at the waist, giving me the perfect view of said bottom as she scrawled something on a piece of paper.

I considered staying longer, but if I did that, she'd think this wasn't just a one-night stand. Girls were complicated like that. If our one night stretched into morning, they got ideas. Ideas that maybe they would be the one to capture the guy no one else could. They would read something more into morning sex than the sex that occurred late at night when both our tongues tasted of beer.

I might sleep around, I might like a variety of ladies, but I never gave false hope where there was none. I might be a dog, but I wasn't an ass.

Sweet Cheeks (I had to call her something) swayed her hips back across the room and held out a scrap of paper to me. "Call me," she said, flipping her hair behind her shoulder.

I glanced at her chest one more time, then stuffed the piece of paper in the front pocket of my jeans.

She leaned up and pressed her lips to mine, slipping her tongue between them. I kissed her back quickly and then slowly pulled away. Reaching around, I palmed her ass. "Thanks for last night," I said and walked out of her bedroom without even looking back.

By the front door, I found my shoes and leather jacket and quickly finished dressing before stepping out into the cold morning air. I wasn't going to miss this cold. I was actually looking forward to moving on, trying something new.

A thin layer of frost covered the windshield of my truck. Instead of getting out and scraping it, I blasted the head and let the engine idle, letting it melt on its own. While I waited, I pulled out the already crumpled piece of paper I was just given. Smoothing it out, I looked down, my eyes skimming over the number I was never going to call to look for her name.

I laughed and crumpled the paper back up and tossed in on the floor of the truck.

Rachel.

Damn. I hadn't even been close.

2

Charlotte

My eyes closed for like the fifth time since I sat down on the couch and turned on the nightly news. With a sigh, I pressed the button on my phone to illuminate the screen and check the time. It was after eleven. He wasn't coming home.

Again.

Really, I wasn't surprised. In fact, it surprised me more that I was sitting here waiting for him. I knew better. Usually, I would just take myself off to bed and not think twice about him being late.

Many nights spent at the office were pretty much required when you were on the fast track to becoming an all-powerful executive. It was common for Max to spend three nights a week at work and then spend many more here at home, working on a laptop into the early hours of the morning. I didn't mind it. I worked a lot too.

A person didn't become successful in their career without sacrifice.

I clicked off the TV and checked to make sure the front door to the apartment was locked. Leaving a small lamp lit in the living room, I headed toward the single bedroom with a yawn. As I walked, I made a mental list of things I needed to accomplish tomorrow and decided that getting up early would be a good idea.

After carrying out my skin care routine and putting on a fresh pair of silk pajamas, I climbed between the crisp, white sheets and laid my head on my pillow. With a final glance at the glowing red numbers on my alarm clock beside the bed, I drifted off into a dreamless sleep.

But sleep didn't last long.

Something woke me. It wasn't necessarily a sound or anything specific. It was a bizarre feeling, something close to intuition that had sleep fading away and consciousness taking over. Even with my eyes still closed, I recognized that it was too dark in here.

The blackness was more penetrating, more final.

I opened my eyes, wanting to confirm what I was feeling. The clock was no longer lit up. The dim light that usually filtered inside the bedroom from the living room was also not there.

The entire apartment was shrouded in darkness and shadow.

My heart began to thump unevenly as panic clawed its way into my chest. *Calm down, Charlotte,* I told myself. *The power is just out. It's not as if that has never happened before.*

Yet something felt off.

Something wasn't right.

Pulling back the covers, I swung my legs over the side of the mattress and stood. Creeping toward the window, I reached for the blinds, meaning to look outside to see how far the power outage reached tonight.

An ear-piercing sound split through the stillness and I shrieked and stumbled backward. My heel caught on the too-long hem of my silk bottoms and I landed on the bed. I lay there feeling my heart pound against my ribs as the fire alarms inside the building shrieked with urgency.

Was there a fire?

Out in the hall of the building, I could hear doors opening and closing, the murmur of voices as people made their way toward the exits.

Great. I guess it wasn't just a false alarm. With a sigh, I pushed up off the bed and grabbed a super soft mohair sweater and slipped my arms through, wrapping it around my middle.

Yeah, technically the fire alarms meant to hurry, but I was in no rush to get outside in the middle of the night, on the sidewalk in the cold. No, thank you.

Navigating the pitch-black apartment shouldn't be a problem; the furniture was always in the exact same spot. I stepped out the bedroom door and walked a few steps down the tiny hallway and into the rest of the apartment.

Where I collided with something hard and large.

What the hell?

I knew for a fact that my furniture was not in this spot.

A large, hot palm wrapped around my upper arm, hooking on like a vise, and jerked me forward. "If you scream, I'll kill you."

I screamed anyway.

I opened my mouth and let out a startled yell as my entire body jerked away from the voice. This was not furniture. This was not good.

His other hand covered my mouth, muffling my scream.

"I said shut up!" he demanded in a harsh whisper, pressing his palm hard against my mouth and jaw. His hand was sweaty and sticky. I wanted to gag.

I held myself stock still, partially in shock. Was there really a fire? Or was the alarm just so thieves could burglarize this building with the distraction of an emergency?

Now I was sorry I didn't hurry down to the sidewalk like everyone else in the building.

The man pulled his hand away from my mouth.

"If you were going to rob the building, you should have done it in the middle of the day when most everyone was at work," I told him.

I felt his stare through the darkness. I could barely make out his features, but he was a large man, likely over six feet and outweighing me by at least fifty pounds. His face pushed in close to mine and his very garlicky breath blew in my face.

"What part of shut up did you not understand?"

My stomach tightened. *Stay calm, Charlotte.* I reminded myself. Staying calm in high-stress situations is what I was trained for. "My purse is on the counter and all my jewelry is in the bedroom. I'm leaving. I won't tell anyone I saw you."

I started to step past him on my way to the door.

I got two steps before he grabbed me.

I didn't think it would be that easy, but at least I tried.

I was jerked off my feet and stumbled back into the solid wall of his body. I felt his breath brush against the back of my ear and little goose bumps of extreme creepiness covered my neck. He leaned close, until I could literally hear the in and out of his nasty mouth breathing.

"I'm not here for your money," he intoned.

He could totally do voiceover for some creepy as hell B-rated movie.

"What are you here for?" I asked, proud that my voice wasn't shaking at all.

He chuckled. It was evil and vile. A shiver started in the balls of my feet and slowly racked my entire body.

"You."

I had two choices. I could:

A)   Dissolve into a puddle of begging and tears

Or

B)   Put the woman's defense class I took to good use.

I brought my bare foot up and slammed it down on the inside of his instep. He was wearing heavy boots and my size-six foot was bare.

He laughed.

I didn't think it was funny.

I threw out my elbow and caught him in the rib. The second I heard the wheeze of pain, I spun around and kicked him in the balls.

He made this little choking sound that I rather enjoyed, and I took off through the darkness toward the door. I wasn't surprised to find the door wasn't even closed. In fact, a slim ray of light showed through the crack. The generators to the building must have been on and illuminating the hallways and powering the elevators.

The fire alarm was still screaming so loudly that my ears were beginning to buzz, as I yanked open the door and plunged into the poorly lit hallway. But at least there was enough light so I could see where I was going.

By now the others had already vacated the floor and I was alone. I ran forward, down the carpeted hallway, passing by numbered apartment doors and bare white walls.

Someone tackled me from behind and I fell face first into the plaid carpeting. Both my arms were pinned behind my back and then a knee held them down. A hard yank on the back of my head brought my face up off the floor, and I looked upward into one of the emergency lights.

"Just for that, I'm going to have to have a little fun with you before I drop you off."

Drop me off? I wasn't a pizza that needed delivered.

I began to struggle beneath him and he yanked harder on my hair, making it scream and burn at the roots. The knee gouging into my back was suddenly gone, and I started to flip, but before I could get around he straddled me, pinning my hands back against me and sinking his crotch right up against them.

Then he swiveled his hips around. "Feel that?" he said crudely. "I'm gonna enjoy getting answers outta you."

I'm pretty sure that was the nastiest thing I'd ever heard. "What answers?" I asked, trying to ignore the grinding hips of the garlic-breath man.

The fire alarm stopped abruptly, but my ears were still ringing. I tried to catch my breath, to come up with a smart plan, to figure a way out of whatever the hell was happening to me.

"Hey, you got her or what?" someone called from down the hall. It was another man. He had a heavy New York accent.

"I got her," garlic breath called.

"Hurry up! Let's go!"

The next thing I knew I was being pulled up from the floor and forced toward the stairwell. The sirens of fire trucks drew near, and I knew that help would be here very soon. I just needed to buy myself a few minutes.

The man shoved me roughly and I threw my hands out to catch my balance, righting myself. But as I moved, I noticed that one of the apartment doors wasn't latched. In their haste, someone forgot to shut their door.

"We gotta go!" the man near the stairwell yelled anxiously as the emergency responders pulled up near the building.

I dropped to the ground, pretending my foot got caught in my pants. I hit my hands and knees and kept my body rigid.

The man above me muttered some profanities and bent down to yank me up.

But I was ready.

As he bent, I threw my body up forcefully. Using my head, I plowed into his chin and jaw, snapping his head back and causing him to grunt. Pain exploded in the back of my skull and I stumbled but quickly focused and pushed away from him and ran at the open door.

Both men shouted as I threw myself inside and slammed the door. I turned the lock just as the handle began to jiggle frantically.

"Open this goddamn door!" the man outside roared.

The other guy with the accent shushed him.

I raced into the kitchen and pulled a giant knife out of the knife block on the counter. If he came in here, I was going to stab him. Then I picked up the phone on the counter and put it to my ear.

No dial tone.

I replaced the receiver and paced back to the door, brandishing the knife like I was in some kind of kitchen death match.

The door handle stopped jingling. The banging on the door went silent. The faint sound of a slamming door at the end of the hall near the stairwell was all I heard.

I gripped the knife tightly and stared at the door. My chest heaved with uneven breath, and the silk pj's stuck to my sweat-slicked skin.

I waited. I watched.

The men had left.

They were gone.

My lungs expelled a great sigh of relief.

Several very long minutes passed until I heard the firemen sweeping through the building, looking for signs of fire.

Tricks

I knew they wouldn't find any.
Whatever the hell just happened had nothing to
do with a fire.

3

Tucker

Everything I owned fit in the back of my pickup truck. The black Dodge was the first thing I bought myself after making it through training and being stationed in North Carolina when I first joined the Corps. Since then, I'd acquired more possessions, but not as many as some of the guys I worked with.

Most of them were married; some were married and divorced and working on a second marriage. Why you would get out of one bad relationship and then dive into another was beyond me. Especially when there were so many ladies out there for sampling.

I mean, I guess I understood to an extent. The Marine Corps wasn't always easy. The hours were long, the pay wasn't that great, and it involved a lot of moving and traveling. Some guys wanted someone to come home to, someone they knew was there waiting for them, missing them.

The problem was when you expected someone to wait and wait and worry for too long, they got tired of it. You can't base a relationship on absence.

I learned that the hard way.

I also learned that one-night stands and quickie flings expelled a lot of loneliness and took care of plenty of my needs without the drama of trying to make sure someone else was happy.

After several years stationed at Camp Lejeune, North Carolina, and a yearlong deployment to a war zone under my belt, I got sent where I am now, Allentown, Pennsylvania. It was a lot quieter here than the other places I'd been, except for that whole business with my friend Nathan and his lady Honor. But that was over, Nathan moved away, and now everything I owned sat boxed in the back of my truck.

After rechecking the tie-down straps over my belongings, I yanked the keys out of my pocket and walked up the stairs to the apartment I shared with two other Marines. They were still at work; they were still enlisted.

I planned to leave the house key on the kitchen counter and then drive away without a glance in the rearview mirror. Just as I was swinging the door around, a black four-door sedan pulled haphazardly into the gravel-filled driveway, blocking in my truck.

Three men in black suits and gray ties stepped out. It reminded me of the movie *Men in Black*. Hell, if it wasn't so overcast today, they would likely be wearing those black sunglasses too.

"I was just about to pull out," I called down to them, hoping they'd get the hint and get the hell out of my way. They could hunt for aliens somewhere else.

"Are you Sergeant Tucker Patton?" one of the men asked, completely ignoring my suggestion he move.

Suspicion laced through me. Immediately I riffled through my memories of last night. Yeah, a lot of it was hazy from all the beer I ingested, but I was almost one hundred percent sure I didn't do anything that would warrant a visit from some cops pretending to be movie stars.

"Who's asking?" I called.

The man who was driving flashed a gold badge with the letters FBI in plain sight across the front.

What the fuck?

The three men proceeded up the steps toward me.

"What's this about?"

"That's him," said one of the men on the steps, like he was somehow able to confirm my identity without me showing him my ID.

"We just need a moment of your time," said the agent closest to me said.

I studied them a moment longer then curiosity got the best of me. It wasn't every day the FBI came a calling. Pushing open the door once more, I motioned them inside.

After closing the door behind us all, I stood there regarding them quietly.

"I'm Agent Collier. Perhaps you should sit down," the man who was driving the car said.

"I'm good where I am." I wasn't about to offer them coffee or tea. I wasn't even going to shake their hands. In fact, the longer I stood in their presence, the more I understood this wasn't going to be a pleasant call.

"We're here on behalf of your brother, Maxwell Patton."

Max was more than just my brother. He was my twin. We were born just minutes apart, me being the "younger" one, and even though we looked exactly the same, our personalities were like night and day. Mom used to joke that someone messed up when they were giving us traits because instead of each having a balanced personality, both of us were extreme.

Max got all the responsible, successful, and determination traits. And me?

I got to be the charming, irresponsible one with a girl on each arm.

It's clear I got the better deal.

It was because of the wide gully of difference between us that Max and I weren't as close as most twins are. I hadn't seen Max since I joined the Corps, but even still I found it very hard—if not impossible—to believe that Max was in trouble with the law.

"Max asked you to come here?" I questioned.

Charged silence filled the space between the agents and me. Tension coiled in the back of my neck, making it feel as if all the muscles and nerves were wound tighter than a double-knotted shoestring.

Agent Collier cleared his throat. "I'm sorry to inform you Maxwell is dead."

The words hit me hard. Shock rippled through my body as disbelief filled my head. There had to be some mistake. Max wasn't dead. He was too young to die. He wasn't even thirty. I snapped my stare back up to the men watching me with solemn expressions.

"Come again?" I asked, thinking I heard wrong.

The man cleared his throat and shifted in his polished black loafers. "It happened last night. It was a car accident."

So I had heard right. An aching hollow feeling opened up in the center of my chest. It settled just beneath my ribs where the pain lodged and continued to hurt. It was the kind of pain no one ever described to me before; I wasn't sure this feeling could be put into words. If it could, they were words no one should ever have to hear.

Suddenly I felt lighter, as if part of whatever held me to the ground was no longer there. I looked down at my feet, at the boots still anchored on the floor. It was strange because it seemed I should be floating.

Part of me was gone.

Ripped away.

Empty.

The hollowness within me flared, and I had to make an effort not to hunch over. I had to work not to let these men in bad suits see how much the death of my twin hurt.

"I'm thinking the FBI usually doesn't make house calls to inform people about their relatives' death."

"Maxwell's death was not an accident."

"You came here to tell me that my brother was murdered?" I asked, deadly calm. I might not have been close to Max, but he was my brother, my family, and I loved him.

"Maxwell was assisting the FBI in a corporate espionage case. He was the inside man. The fact that he was working with us was kept under wraps."

"Obviously not if someone killed him because of it."

The silence that followed my statement filled the room. If these men thought they could come here, tell me that my brother died helping them, and not be met with some sort of angry animosity, they seriously did not know who they were dealing with.

The fact that Max had been doing this at all surprised me. Part of me wanted to ask if they were sure they had the right guy, but respect kept the question in. Respect for my brother. Just because it was out of character for Max to get involved in something like this didn't mean he hadn't. He was a hard-working guy, always on the straight and narrow path. He never strayed from his goals; he never had time for fun or anything he considered time wasters.

But he did have a strong sense of right and wrong.

That was likely the only personality quality we shared.

So yeah, it might be unlikely that Max would become involved in some sort of criminal case, but it wasn't impossible. Especially if whatever was going on had been blocking the path he was traveling.

Respect for him rose up inside me like a bottle of shaken soda. That hollow feeling threatened to pull me under and grief was a pungent taste in the back of my throat.

He can't be gone.

He's too young to die.

The man across from me cleared his throat. "No one knows of Maxwell's passing. You're the only one who's been told."

I swallowed thickly, pushing down the bubbly emotion inside me. I thought about my mother, my father, my sister. I was going to shatter their world today. I swallowed again. "I'll take care of it," I told them.

They said nothing, but I felt the change in the room. I looked up, directly into the eyes of one of the agents. There was a reason I was being told first. There was a reason that no one else had been notified about his death.

"The accident scene?" I asked.

"Has been cleaned up."

Yeah, there was definitely something more going on.

"Sergeant, right before your brother died, he spoke to us."

"What did he say?" *What were the last words my brother would ever speak?*

"He told us to get you. To get Tucker."

He asked for me. Max's last thought, his last request was of me.

Suddenly I understood the man's words. *That's him.* Of course they knew it was me on sight. I looked exactly like Max. We shared the same face.

"We need you to step in where Maxwell left off. To assume the identity of your brother."

It was crazy. It would never work. People would know the minute I opened my mouth that I wasn't Max.

Perhaps the look on my face made the men think I was going to say no.

"This case has been ongoing for over a year. If you don't help, all the work we've done will have been for nothing. These men will walk."

"Those men killed my brother," I said. A sense of revenge overcame me.

No one said anything.

Tricks

No one but me.
"I'll do it."

4

Charlotte

If there was one stereotype that I hated above all others it was that all blondes were dumb. Born a natural blonde I fought against the stereotype my entire life. I even considered dying my hair brown, but that would be like admitting defeat or trying to hide who I really am to appease some people with large mouths that had tendencies to act like assholes.

Besides, I was a walking testament that blondes weren't dumb.

Plus, brown hair would totally wash me out.

Once I was certain Garlic Breath and his friend were gone, I slipped out of my neighbor's apartment (They needed a class in organization and hoarding) back into the hallway. I could hear the emergency responders clanking up the stairwell and I experienced a moment of panic.

Then I realized I hadn't done anything wrong.

Well, except for fail to vacate a building that was potentially burning to the ground.

I rushed back into my place just as the door to the stairwell burst open and men filed into the hallway.

I knew what I had to do.

I removed the clip from my hair and shook out the blond strands so they appeared messy and slept on. I never walked around with bed head, but desperate times called for desperate measures.

Opening the door to my apartment, I stumbled out into the hallway, faking a yawn and rubbing at my eyes like I was still half asleep.

The men in the hallway all stopped and stared at me.

"What's going on?" I asked, trying to sound tired. In my opinion, I sounded like someone doing a poor imitation of a drunk person.

"What are you doing here, ma'am?"

Great. Not only was I a dumb blonde with uncombed hair today, but I was also a *ma'am*. I should wander down to the social security office and apply for my senior citizen card while I was at it.

"I live here," I said, blinking my eyes at them like I was confused. Then I gazed over their fire suits and equipment. "Is there a fire?"

"Didn't you hear the alarm?" one of the other guys asked, amusement clear in his tone.

"I sleep with headphones and a noise machine," I said. "A girl has to get her beauty sleep."

God. I sounded like a complete twit.

"We're going to have to ask you to vacate the building while we finish searching the area."

I nodded. "Of course." I gestured to my apartment. "That one's mine. There's no fire in there."

I pulled the door closed, hoping they didn't go looking for the noise machine I claimed to sleep with. One of the men held open the door for me and, okay, yeah, I might have peeked at his physique. He was a fireman, a good-looking one at that.

I heard the men laugh as the door closed behind me. I breathed a massive sigh of relief I wasn't asked more questions. I wasn't sure I was ready to tell people what happened to me. I wanted to think it through. I wanted to weigh the situation in my mind, think of all the possibilities of what went on tonight.

Downstairs in the lobby, cold air swirled inside from the door leading onto the sidewalk. I slowed my steps. I was supposed to go out there, but I wasn't wearing any socks or shoes. I'd have frostbite in minutes. New York City in late January could be brutal. The wind, the snow, the low temperatures, and this winter was supposed to be very long and anything but mild.

And if I somehow avoided frostbite, I would get some weird disease walking on the bare sidewalk of the city. My skin crawled just thinking about what could be growing out there.

A few of the people who lived in the building still loitered just inside the door so I took up position beside them. I scanned the faces—not for anyone familiar, but for two men who seemed like they might not belong.

I didn't get a great look at the men from upstairs, but I knew if I saw Garlic Breath again I would know him. He wasn't in sight, not inside and not outside in the crush of people on the sidewalk.

What did that mean?

What are you here for?

You.

His whispered one-word reply caused goose bumps to break out over my arms and legs. Why would he say that? What could he possibly want with me?

"Stupid kids," someone next to me muttered. "What's this city coming to?"

"What do you mean?" I asked before I could remind myself he probably hadn't been talking to me.

"Didn't you hear?"

I shook my head. "I slept through most of this." I gestured at the crowd, the officers, and the fire truck parked out at the curb.

The woman on the other side of the man chuckled. "Ah, to be young again. I used to be able to sleep through anything too. Now I'm lucky to get four hours straight."

The man in the center of us nodded empathetically. They were an older married couple, both with graying hair and wrinkles on the outer corners of their eyes.

"It appears some kids pulled the fire alarms and waited 'til people started evacuating to enter some apartments and rob them."

My first thought upon hearing this news was disbelief. That wasn't what happened here tonight...

Was it?

"Who said that's what happened?"

The man gave me a strange look before replying. "The police." He motioned outside where two officers in blue uniforms were talking to some of the people I recognized from living in the building. "Seems the kids only burglarized the first floor. They didn't have time for the rest."

Is that was Garlic Breath and his friend were doing? Hoping to make easy money in the midst of chaos they themselves created? I hadn't gotten a great look at them, but I knew they weren't kids.

Of course the firemen upstairs called me ma'am and this woman down here was wishing she was as young as me. Clearly everyone had their own definition of age.

I was thinking in circles. That never happened. Usually I was analytical and concise with my thoughts. I was just tired, in shock, and yeah, okay… maybe I was a little scared.

I found myself wishing that Max were here. It would be nice to not be alone tonight.

I turned back to the man, to hopefully draw some more information out of him, when one of the officers stepped inside. All his attention was on me.

"Ma'am," he said. "We'll need to get your statement."

"Of course," I agreed and turned away from the older couple to give him my full attention.

I started to explain why I was late, but he cut me off to ask, "Did you see anyone in the building? Anyone who seemed liked they didn't belong?"

"Is this about the robberies?" I questioned. A good lawyer always answered a question with one of her own.

He nodded briskly. "We're trying to gain descriptions from all those who might have seen them as they were vacating the building."

"I was late vacating. I wear headphones at night." The lie was easier to tell, like once I had gotten over telling it upstairs, it no longer mattered. I wondered if that's how criminals felt. Like after their first crime, the ones after it didn't even matter.

"Did you see anyone on your way out? Anyone you didn't recognize? Anyone who was acting suspicious?"

I thought about Garlic Breath and the way he seemed to just appear in my dark apartment. I thought about how he wasn't interested in any of my material possessions, not even after I told him he could have them.

I thought for long moments.

And then I lied again.

"No. The only people I saw were the firemen, clearing the building."

The officer seemed disappointed, but he didn't question my statement. After a few more general questions and my brief explanation of how I saw nothing at all, the officer moved on to the next interviewee.

I never lied. Lying only got people in trouble, a fact I saw day after day in my job as a lawyer.

But I just lied tonight. To an officer of the law no less.

Why?

Something inside me told me to keep my mouth shut.

5

Tucker

The entire drive from Pennsylvania to New York City was spent sitting in the back of a black SUV and being briefed on my brother's life. In order to be able to pull off literally stepping into his shoes, I had to know as much as I could about him.

I think the Feds assumed I knew more than I did. I didn't bother to correct them. In truth, I was mildly embarrassed that I didn't know more about Max and his life these days. Every detail they told me seemed to affect me in one way or another. I felt amused at how focused and intent on success Max was, but that wasn't to say I wasn't impressed. Max was achieving his goals. I never doubted he would.

As we drove, I was handed countless items, like a driver's license with Max's name on it, a cell phone programmed with his contacts, the keys to his apartment, and bank cards with his name on them as well.

It seemed wrong to touch the money that belonged to my brother. It wasn't rightfully mine and likely it was all willed to our parents. When I tried to refuse, I was met with stone-cold silence and looks of disapproval.

I almost laughed.

Like I gave a damn if they liked me or not.

"Take the cards," the man to my left finally said. He must have realized that I don't bow under pressure. "The guys who wanted Max dead think he's dead. When you show up, they're going to be shocked and probably suspicious. If you start using a different bank or anything that even seems simple, they're gonna know."

I put the bank card and the other IDs into my leather jacket pocket.

The man to my right cleared his throat. "Be sure to use Max's closet. He, uh, never wore leather jackets."

"I'll do my job," I said, leaving no room for any more orders they wanted to present as suggestions. I probably wanted the men the Feds were after more than they did. This was just a case to them, a check in the box, a job well done.

Not to me.

To me, this was my brother's life.

This was justice.

The city came into view, with sky-sweeping buildings, crowded streets, and cluttered sidewalks. People bustled around wrapped up in coats and scarves. Some carried briefcases; some carried white cups with the infamous green logo on the front. The coffee that came in those cups was apparently available on every single block in this monster of a city.

We had only been traveling for a short time, but the difference between New York City and the town in Pennsylvania where I was coming from were very different. There was an energy to this city, a hum of activity that I would bet never went to bed. Blaring horns and smells from the many vendors on the sidewalks all pressed in on me, making me feel like I was in a different world.

"Have you been to the city before?" one of the men asked me as I stared out the window.

"Not since I was a kid." I might as well have never been here before. Seeing something through the eyes of a child was never the same as through the eyes of the grown man.

The man started talking again, telling me all of Max's usual places—the coffee shop he visited every morning, the restaurants he frequented.

I made a sound and the man stopped talking. "I'm surprised my brother went out to eat. I figured he would be eating at his desk."

The men in the car exchanged a look.

"What?" I said, knowing immediately that there was something I was missing.

The SUV slid up to the curb in front of a towering apartment building made of cream-colored stone.

"This is your apartment."

"Max's apartment," I corrected.

"Remember," Black suit number three said. "We need you to find the thumb drive that Max had in his possession. It contains records and statements that will put away many powerful men for a very long time."

"How do you know it didn't get destroyed in the car crash that killed my brother?"

"He told us it was somewhere safe."

I felt a pang of sorrow for my brother. For his loss. I wished he was somewhere safe.

I palmed the keys to the apartment and prepared to get out of the car. I needed some air. I needed some time to think. To grieve.

"Do not confront the men who killed Max. They will get their punishment. Don't do anything that might make anyone suspicious of who you really are. Find the thumb drive, contact us, and then you can bury your brother the way he deserved."

I swung around. "You have his body?"

The man beside me grimaced. "There wasn't much left."

So there would be no burying of my brother. He was cheated out of life and a proper funeral. Anger inflamed my insides, sweeping through me like a raging fire. I wanted to punch something.

I started to get out of the SUV.

"Wait," one of the men in black said behind me. "You do know that your brother didn't live alone."

It wasn't really a question; it was said more like a statement, like a confirmation of knowledge already known.

A feeling of thick dread dropped into my gut. "No."

"For the past year, your brother has been living with someone."

"He has a roommate," I said, really hoping that's what they meant.

The man cleared his throat. "Girlfriend."

Fuck.

"So I'm supposed to play boyfriend to…" My voice trailed away as I realized I didn't know the name of the woman who was living with my only brother.

"Charlotte Rose Carter," he supplied. "We realize this might be uncomfortable."

I made a sound the boys in the Corps taught me. It wasn't polite. They wanted me to go up there and pretend to be someone else, to look into the eyes of a woman who loved my brother and who was now going to be betrayed. She would just go about her day like he wasn't even gone, like all was right with the world, when really everything was all wrong.

"It isn't as if we are asking you to sleep with her," the man said.

I barked a laugh. Sleeping with my brother's woman was the last thing on my mind.

"I'll be in touch when I have the drive," I said shortly. I was beyond done with this conversation. I realized these men were just trying to do their jobs, but they were assholes.

I slammed the door to the SUV the second my feet hit the sidewalk. They disappeared into the New York traffic seconds later. I took a deep breath and stared up at the building. Cold air whipped around, pushing against my skin and hair. I didn't mind the cold. It was a good way to help numb that hollow ache in the center of my chest.

Not quite ready to go inside, I pulled out the phone I was given and dialed a number I knew from memory. As the line rang, I stepped closer to the building, realizing someone might recognize me if I hung out in the middle of the sidewalk.

"This is Reed." A voice came on the line.

"It's Patton."

"Patton? Why didn't you call from your phone?" Nathan and I had been friends since being stationed together a couple years ago. It really hadn't been that long, but it was long enough for us to recognize that we were cut from the same cloth. Nathan and I shared the same experiences, the same hobbies, the same Marine Corps mentality that many of the men we worked with displayed.

The instant alert was clear in his tone, the instant urge to rush into action when he felt something wasn't right. We read each other well. It was that coupled with everything else that made us tight. Hell, it made us honorary brothers.

"It's a long story," I explained, not wanting to get into everything out here in the open. "I'm in NYC, family stuff. Can you hold the job for me until I can get down to North Carolina?"

Nathan pulled the phone down so his voice was slightly muffled. "Patton wants me to hold his job," he said with a hint of humor in his tone.

I couldn't help but smile. Honor, Nathan's wife came onto the line. "Patton have you gotten yourself in trouble already?"

"You know it."

She laughed, but then her voice turned serious. "Call if you need him."

By *him*, I knew she meant Nathan. A guy would think after everything she had been through, she wouldn't want Nathan involved in anything dangerous. It just goes to show how tough Honor really was.

"Thanks," I replied, and I meant it.

Seconds later, Nathan was back on the line. "What can I do?" he said, his tone serious.

"I got it handled."

"I have no doubt, man," he said. "You know you got a place here. I'll just sweet talk Honor out from behind that computer and she can help me with the first couple cases."

I heard Honor's giggle in the background and rolled my eyes. Those two were enough to give a guy cavities. Everyone knew I liked women, but settling down with just one? Wasn't going to happen.

"We got work already?" I said, surprise and pride swelling in me. When Nathan first invited me down to Jacksonville to be part of a private investigation firm, I knew it was something I wanted to do. I just hoped we could make it work.

"Yep. We got some contracts with the Corps already."

"Sweet." A pang of regret hit me because I wanted to be there. But this was important. This was for my brother.

"You're sure you're all good?" Nathan asked, reading me again, even from over the phone. Sometimes that guy was so perceptive it was creepy.

"All good."

"Call me if that changes."

After I agreed, we both hung up and I pushed the phone back into my pocket and stared down at the new keys to my new apartment.

The apartment I now shared with my brother's girlfriend.

6

Charlotte

The hot water slid over my bare skin, leaving a trail of tingles along my flesh and causing a deep moan to vibrate my throat.

There wasn't anything quite like a steaming hot shower to release the tension that always seemed to find its way into my muscles during the day. Massages were good too, but who had time for that?

Stepping backward under the spray, water cascaded over my head, weighing my hair down and pressing the silky strands against my back. I pushed the remaining conditioner through the ends of my hair and as the product made its way down to the drain, I closed my eyes and took a deep breath.

How I wished I could slip into a pair of satin pajamas and curl up on the end of the couch, maybe with some movie from my high school days that we all used to giggle over in the theater while eating gummy bears and Sour Patch Kids.

There would be no silly movie, candy, or even lounging in pajamas for me tonight. I had to work.

The only reason I was home was because I wanted to change before meeting a client for dinner at one of the cafés near Times Square.

It was a new case, a new client, and I got the "privilege" of making sure they signed with Keller, Krane, and Associates. As I stood under the cooling spray, lingering in the quiet of the shower, I reminded myself this dinner, this meeting was just one more way I could improve my standing at the firm. It was one more way I could prove my worth to the partners and solidify my position.

I'd been working toward this for as long as I could remember. Being a success was my dream, my life's work.

So why did I feel so tired?

I shut off the water and grabbed the white towel hanging over the shower curtain bar. After half drying I stepped out onto the white rug in front of the mirror and swiped my hand across the fogged-up glass. My hand mark was just enough to see my reflection in the mirror.

After smoothing some leave-in conditioner in the tangled mess that was unfortunately my hair, I began working out the tangles with a wide-tooth comb.

Maybe my exhaustion was just because I barely slept last night. Waking up to a piercing alarm and a creepy man in my apartment, who then proceeded to try and kidnap me, was enough to make anyone tired.

Not to mention I spent my entire day reliving what happened and going over every detail in my head, over and over again. Several times I found myself reaching for the phone to call the officer I spoke to down in the lobby, but every time I changed my mind.

It wasn't as if I thought I misunderstood what happened to me; it was quite the opposite. I understood quite clearly that those "break-ins" on the lower floor and the fire alarm had merely been a distraction. A distraction to get to what they really wanted.

Me.

What I didn't understand was why.

And being the analytical, goal-oriented person that I was, I knew I couldn't just call the police and tell them my suspicions without something more. I was curious by nature.

Curiosity killed the cat. The thought echoed through my head like some childhood nursery rhyme.

Good thing I wasn't a cat.

I laid down the comb and reached for a jar of moisturizer when a sound had my movements freezing. I stood there completely still while my heartbeat jack hammered beneath my ribcage. Images from last night flashed behind my eyes. A man creeping through the dark. A sweaty palm grabbing me. The absolute feeling of panic clawing its way up my windpipe.

I locked the door when I came home.

Hadn't I?

I glanced on the counter for my cell phone. Screw not calling the cops. But my cell wasn't in the bathroom. It was lying useless in the bottom of my purse out in the kitchen.

I wondered what was worse: having your dead body discovered wearing granny panties or no panties at all…?

Another sound came from out in the living room. I cocked my head to the side, trying to figure out what it was. But I didn't know.

Yelling for help would only alert the intruder I knew he was there.

There was only one thing I could do.

Swallowing down my fear, I tightened the towel around me and reached for the handle on the door.

I was going out there.

Tucker

I was hoping she wasn't going to be home.

Soon as I let myself into the apartment, I heard the shower running and knew that she was.

I probably should have taken the time to ask for more information about her. Like what she did for a living. Surely she had a job, but I didn't know what it was. It would have been helpful in figuring out her daily schedule and hours. But it was too late now.

I didn't ask and I couldn't bring myself to really think much about it. This wasn't about her. I didn't need to know her to get this job done. In fact, the less I knew about her, the less I saw of her, the better it would be for everyone.

My eyes took in the room, focusing on the small but clean space. This is where my brother lived. This was where he spent his free time and his nights.

That insistent ache in my chest intensified and my heart squeezed. This was hard. Harder than I thought it would be. Not only was I staring at my brother's life, but the life I knew nothing about. My own brother.

How could I let so many years pass without reaching out to him?

I'm sorry, Max.

Shutting the door silently behind me, I stepped farther into the room, my eyes taking in everything but really only wanting to see one thing.

You'd think I wouldn't really need to see a photo of my brother, being that we shared the same face, but it wasn't really someone's features that make them who they are completely. I think I understood that better than most people because I did share my face. Yet Max and I… we wore them so differently.

Hopefully I would find the flash drive before anyone figured that out.

I skimmed the surfaces of the room, the coffee table, the small wooden bookshelf crammed with books. The generic art hanging on the walls of scenic views and ocean waves. The couch was solid gray with a few white pillows on each end and small round side tables flanked each end. The only thing on the tables was one lamp each.

There were no framed photos. No smiling couple images. Nothing really that told of the people who lived here. There were no hobby magazines. There were no movie cases on the stand beneath the flat screen.

I never stayed in the same place very long because of the Corps, but even I had stuff lying around that would have given some clue to the kind of guy I was.

I wandered over to the bookcase and leaned down, looking at the rows of books filling up the shelves. Most of them were on law and business.

Was this woman a lawyer?

Great. Just what I needed. Some opinionated, nosy, question-filled woman that was going to argue and pick apart every last thing I said.

Or maybe the books had been my brother's. Maybe he had been brushing up on the law because of the things he was involved in. God, I hoped so. I did not want to deal with a lawyer right now. I stood up and looked behind me at the bar separating the living area from the kitchen. A brown leather purse was lying there atop a black briefcase.

I would find answers about this chick in there. I rushed across the room and in my haste, I bumped into the table and knocked it over. With a light swear, I caught it, but not before the lamp hit the carpet. It was made of silver metal so thankfully it hadn't broken.

I picked up the lamp and the shade fell off, hitting the floor again. I swore a manly type of swear and then scooped it up and slid it into place.

What the hell does a man need a lamp for anyway? That's what the lights in the ceilings were for.

I started toward the bag on the counter once more when the door across the room swung open and a woman came barreling out. She was nothing but a blur of movement, forcefully rushing forward as a cry of determination ripped from her throat.

Before I could ask her what the hell all the excitement was about, she tackled me.

She freaking tackled me to the floor.

We landed on the carpet in a heap, with me beneath her and a pair of long, tan legs straddling my middle.

Her legs were bare.

Holy mother of God, she was wearing nothing but a towel.

She was wet. She was mostly naked. *She was sitting across my lap*.

Desire swelled inside me and all thought left my head. I couldn't even be shocked she managed to tackle me because I was too busy thinking about the weight of her across my hips. Damn, she felt delicious.

My body started to react on its own; it never needed any prompting from me. In fact, I have gotten hard from a lot less than something like this. I blinked, trying to focus on the fact she clearly meant me bodily harm.

Was my brother into this kinky shit?

Maybe he hadn't been as straight-laced as I thought…

As I considered the possibility of this woman gyrating her hips on top of me and demanding I get out of my clothes, she drew her arm back and swung down.

Thank God I had reflexes that were just as automatic as the hardening of my dick.

My hand caught her wrist just before she clobbered me with something.

"What the fuck!" I yelled, snapping out of my sex dream and back to reality. I blinked, looking at what I just stopped from hitting me upside the head.

It was a giant-ass hairbrush. It was large and round with bristles that actually looked like they would leave a mark if she got in a good swing. And judging from her actions just seconds before, if I had been any slower on the uptake, I'd be sporting a rash from that thing and a headache.

"Max!" the hairbrush-yielding she-devil exclaimed. She released the grip on the brush and it fell from her grasp, hitting me right in the nose.

"Goddamn it!" I roared and knocked it away, where it hit the bottom of the island with a thud.

"I'm sorry!" she gasped, reaching down to grab my face and inspect where the brush hit.

Our eyes collided.

For long seconds, time stood still.

In that fleeting moment I realized two things:

1)   Clearly this wasn't a time of day when Max would be home.

And

2)   Her eyes were fucking gorgeous.

They were round and wide, almost innocent. Hazel-colored orbs stared down at me, and from this distance I could make out the green and gold flecks that swam around, combining to make a color unique to the wearer. The outside edges were trimmed with a forest green, the kind of green that I only ever saw when living in Pennsylvania. It was the kind of green that bloomed deep in the forest, a natural green that up until now I thought only Mother Nature could create.

The almond shape of her eyes was rimmed with gold-colored lashes, long and sweeping, that turned up at the outside corners.

"Do you always greet Max like this when he comes home?" I asked, the words literally falling from my lips before I could even think about what I was saying.

A single drop of water dripped from the end of her cascading hair and splashed on my cheek, instantly rolling down the side of my jaw.

The action seemed to break whatever the hell was happening.

She wrinkled her brow and used her thumb to wipe away the rogue drop of water. "What did you say?" she asked, straightening up when the water was gone.

My eyes slipped down to her chest, where the white towel wrapped around her body was coming loose.

It wasn't a very big towel.

I stared at her and the blood in my veins began to move faster, began to furiously make its way downward into the controlling force inside my jeans. Her hair was long and damp; it tangled around her face and strands clung to her shoulders like Velcro.

Damn, her skin was smooth. And wet. I watched with apt attention as another drop of water escaped the strands and slid downward, leaving a damp trail over the swell of her breast and disappearing beneath the white cloth.

"Max?" she asked, reminding me that she was waiting for an answer. Her voice was breathless and the raspiness of it brushed over my senses, setting my cock to throbbing.

My hands itched to slide up the inside of her thighs and tug away the towel so I could feast in all her naked glory. I cleared my throat. "I said I wasn't expecting you to be home," I finally answered, hoping to God that what I was saying was actually accurate.

I needed to get this woman off me. STAT. The only brain that was operating right now was the one in my pants. Usually, I liked it that way, but this wasn't a good time.

This was my brother's woman.

Shit.

"I have a business meeting over dinner and I wanted to change before I met the client." she replied with a nod.

Wrapping my hands around her narrow waist, I lifted her up, off my lap, and set her aside. Her mouth formed a little O of surprise, and I wondered what the hell I was doing that was so O-worthy.

I smirked. It wasn't the first time I'd seen that face. All chicks thought I was O-worthy at one time or another.

"You scared the crap out of me!" she said, a relived giggle in her tone.

"I didn't mean to," I said, getting up off the floor and turning toward the kitchen. When I went around the island, I discreetly shifted the stiff junk in my jeans and hoped it would go down before she noticed. Keeping my back turned, I went toward the fridge. I needed a beer.

There weren't any.

Lamps and fridges without beer. Was this the fucking *Twilight Zone?*

I grabbed a bottled water (It was that or Snapple. What man actually drank Snapple?) and twisted the cap, shooting it into the sink like a basketball. I took a long drink and realized the silence in the room was a little intense.

I looked over, wiping my mouth with the back of my hand. She had come closer. What the hell was her name again? She was only gripping the towel closed with one hand, and I thought about telling her to go get dressed. I mean, what the hell kind of woman just parades around wet and practically naked?

A woman who thinks she's at home with her man.

Her eyes were wide as she took me in, and I realized that I was still wearing my clothes. Clothes I knew Max would likely not be caught dead in.

"Where did you get those clothes?" she asked, starting at my feet, taking in my ratty jeans, T-shirt, and black leather jacket.

Yep. She had to be a lawyer.

"I borrowed them from someone at work."

Her light-colored eyebrow rose in defiance. "Someone at the office wears jeans and leather?"

I shrugged. It was the best I could do.

"Did you get your hair cut?" she asked, studying me anew.

I set the water on the counter and ran my palm over the top of my head. Of course my hair was shorter than Max's. Mine had to be short because of the Corps. I was out now so I could let it grow, but it was a habit to keep it short.

"Yeah. I thought it would be easier, you know, with my schedule," I said, hoping she believed me.

"It looks good on you." She gave me a small smile. A gentle lift to her full, heart-shaped mouth. Thoroughly kissable lips.

Mentally, I gave myself a slap. *Knock it off! This is your brother's woman!* the brain in my head screamed, thankfully taking over the situation.

"Thanks," I rasped, giving all the attention to the icy-cold water bottle on the counter.

"Did you get any sleep last night at all?"

Where did she think I was all night? She didn't seem worried, not at all. It kind of ticked me off. She should be worried, frantic even, that Max hadn't come home last night. I mean, shit, it was late afternoon and she'd still heard nothing from him. Yet here she was, taking a shower and getting ready to go out to dinner. I snatched the water up and took a long sip, hoping to clamp down on my irritation. I knew for sure that Max wasn't the kind to get irritated easily. I was the hothead, not him.

Behind me I heard her move into the kitchen, her bare feet barely making a sound against the tile. I turned as she reached out and took the bottle of water I had just been drinking out of. I watched her heart-shaped lips wrap around the bottle as she took a dainty sip.

Just when I thought I was gaining control of the situation, she went and used her lips. On my bottle. "I know sleeping in your office isn't the most ideal place," she replied.

So she thought I spent the night at work. She wasn't surprised either. Was this a normal thing?

I nodded. "I got a couple hours. Then I spilled coffee all over my suit and had to borrow a change of clothes."

"Do you have to go back in?" She shifted and some light floral scent wafted toward me. She smelled good. Fresh and… calm.

I never knew a person could smell calm. She had this quietness about her; not quiet in a literal sense, but in figurative way. In a stable way. Like if she were an electrical panel, she would be the grounding wire. She would be the wire that would keep the other wires around her from electrocuting everyone they came into contact with.

The irritation I was feeling moments before ebbed away and I was left feeling composed. "No, I'm not going back to work tonight." I ignored the fact my voice dropped an octave.

Her impossibly wide eyes widened even more. Was she that surprised I wasn't planning on rushing back to work? Had I already done the wrong thing?

Before I could make an attempt to fix whatever the hell I just did, the sound of a ringing phone nearby had her reaching into the brown bag on the counter. I watched as she held the black encased phone up to her ear.

"This is Charlotte Carter."

Charlotte! That was her name!

"Yes," she was saying. "I see, yes, of course. Tomorrow is just fine…"

She kept talking, but I stopped listening as my gaze wandered down her body and to her legs again. Her toes were painted red.

It was sexy.

She sighed and pulled the phone away from her, setting it on the counter.

"Everything okay?" I asked, forcing my gaze up.

"The client had to reschedule for tomorrow."

"So you get to play hooky?"

She got this funny look on her face and she glanced at me. Then she said, "I suppose so."

"We can have dinner, then," I said. I hadn't planned on dinner with her. I planned on spending as little time as possible with her.

But that was before she tackled me, half naked, and calmed me with a single look from her golden lash-lined eyes.

Besides, I could use this dinner as an investigation of sorts. This woman—Charlotte—lived with my brother. Maybe I could learn things that would help me nail the fucktards who murdered my twin. Maybe she knew where the flash drive was.

"Dinner?" she asked. The way she said it made me think this suggestion was a surprise. Did my brother never take her out to eat?

I shrugged. "I'm off. You're off. I'm starving. You're thin. You could use a meal. Let's eat together."

Judging by the look on her face, I went and said something un-Max-like again. Damn, being someone else was hard.

"You think I'm too thin?"

Well, shit. Not only did I say something out of character, but I committed the cardinal sin that every man knew to never commit. I commented on a woman's weight.

I decided to blame it on the twilight zone atmosphere of this tiny apartment.

I sighed heavily. "I don't think you're too thin. I think you're gorgeous. Go get dressed so we can go."

Her face softened and she smiled. "Okay."

Well, that was easy.

Before going off to find some pants—*Please, God, let her cover up those legs*—she tilted her head to the side. "Aren't you going to change?"

Right.

It was time to trade my leather jacket for something far less comfortable. "Of course." I followed along behind her, toward the bedroom, which was just off the living room.

My cock was twitching again because I was envisioning both of us in the bedroom getting dressed...

Charlotte didn't go into the bedroom, instead veering back into the bathroom. "I'll be ready in a few minutes," she called as she closed the door behind her.

My shoulders sagged in relief as I stepped into the bedroom. I couldn't help but look at the bed, the very large bed that dominated the room.

I pictured Charlotte's long, bare legs and peek-a-boo chest. I was supposed to share a bed with that and not touch it. I'd never shared a bed with a woman I didn't plan on touching.

It was going to be a very long night.

8

Charlotte

I leaned against the bathroom door, pressing a hand against my chest as if the movement would somehow calm my racing heart. The rapid rhythm against my palm only served to remind me how worked up I was.

When had my life become so crazy that when faced with a noise in the other room, I immediately thought it was an intruder instead of the other person who actually lived here?

I pushed away from the door and stepped in front of the mirror and looked at my reflection. My cheeks were flushed, my eyes bright. My hair looked like someone took an egg beater and twirled it around on my head on the highest speed it could go.

Get control of yourself, Charlotte! I demanded of myself. *It wasn't an intruder.*

So why had my body reacted with such surprise when I saw Max? It was almost as if my brain hadn't recognized him right away. I had been about to clobber him with my hairbrush. He likely thought I was insane because I'd never acted so impulsively in the year we'd been together.

Last night freaked me out more than I realized. It altered the way I reacted to situations. It made me feel less in control. It made me feel more vulnerable. It seemed silly that an "almost" kidnapping could have such an effect on me. I was mildly embarrassed. I mean, I practically attacked poor Max.

He didn't seem to mind… a voice whispered in the back of my mind.

The flush already in my cheeks deepened and I glanced around the room as if to make sure no one was watching me. I felt as if I'd been caught doing something I wasn't supposed to be doing. A little thrill coursed through my body. Judging from the solid length I felt against my thigh earlier, Max *definitely* hadn't minded my attack. His reaction surprised me. I'd never thought he was the kind of guy to get so turned on so fast.

He seemed different tonight, starting with the way he looked. The shorter hairstyle defined his jaw, making it look more square, his features more angular. It also looked like he hadn't shaved that morning, which was very unlike him.

And then there were his clothes. The outfit was definitely borrowed because Max didn't dress that way; he was a suit and tie kind of guy. But tonight worn-out blue jeans hung low on his hips, loose and relaxed. The jeans he usually wore were dark, crisp, and fitted. The leather jacket was also worn looking and hugged his upper body like it might be a little too snug, but instead of making the jacket look too small, it made him appear broad and built.

And his grip… dear God, his grip. The way he palmed my waist and lifted me off him like I weighed nothing at all had been… Well, it had been sexy. Max never manhandled me in any way. He was also so respectful, so careful of me, like I might break. Those were things about him I always thought were sweet and gentlemanly. But tonight, he hadn't been sweet.

I liked it.

Clearly, last night's events affected me way more than I realized. Aside from becoming a paranoid overreactor I had also become… Well, I wasn't sure. But if I kept standing here scrutinizing everything I felt, I was never going to be ready for dinner.

For the first time in a long time I felt a little giddy rush at the thought of a dinner date. I no longer wanted to curl up with a movie in a pair of pj's. The thought of going out to dinner with Max was exciting. It wasn't as if it was the first time we'd gone out, but tonight felt different.

After re-combing my hair and blasting the long strands with the blow dryer and applying a quick five-minute makeup routine, I dressed in the panties, bra, and camisole I took in the bathroom with me. Then I smoothed my tangle-prone, thin strands back into a neat bun at the base of my neck.

I stepped into the bedroom with anticipation coiling low in my abdomen. My eyes immediately went to his side of the closet, where I was hoping to see him standing.

The room was empty.

Feeling the sharp sting of disappointment, I quickly dressed in a black pencil skirt, a white silk top, and a black fitted jacket. After slipping into a pair of black heels, I went out into the living room in search of Max.

He was sprawled—not sitting, but *sprawled*—across the sofa, making the couch seem much smaller than it actually was. Both his arms were thrown out across the back, one leg was up on the coffee table, and one was flung out with his foot resting on the floor.

I'd never seen him appear so relaxed. The first thing I thought was that he was going to wrinkle the suit he was wearing.

"Are you watching the sports channel?" I asked, taking in his appearance once more.

He sat up abruptly and flipped off the television. "It was the news, but they were talking about the game," he replied, standing up.

I forgot about sports.

The suit he was wearing wasn't anything I hadn't seen before. In fact, it was just a regular navy suit with a jacket and matching slacks.

But the way he was wearing it… It looked new.

The jacket seemed to hug his shoulders a little more closely than before. The pants clung to the thickness of his thighs instead of falling away. And he wasn't wearing a tie. The white dress shirt was left open at the throat, exposing the smooth skin of his neck and throat.

He still hadn't shaved.

The contrast of his rough-textured jaw against the sleek lines of his suit was… stunning.

Just when I thought my heart rate was back in control, it began to beat unevenly once more. I swallowed thickly, unable to tear my gaze away from the hollow of his throat.

"You ready?" Max asked. Something in his tone made me look up into his chocolate eyes.

I cleared my throat and composed myself. "Yes."

"Where do you want to go?" he asked, holding open the apartment door for me as I grabbed my purse off the counter.

I started to reply, stepping around him and into the hallway, when the dark shape of a man rushing me caught my attention.

Flashes of last night assaulted me and with a squeal, I stumbled backward, trying to get away. The heel of my black pump snapped with a cracking sound, causing my already teetering frame to buckle and fall.

Solid arms wrapped around me from behind, and an unyielding chest stopped me from falling any farther.

"Whoa there," he said, his voice right beside my ear, and the deep baritone in which he spoke caused the nerves in the back of my neck to tingle with awareness. "I got you."

And he did. It was like his body had become my safety net and I knew that as long as his arms were around me, nothing bad was going to happen.

The man who was barreling toward me kept going, his muttered curse following along behind him as he went. I watched, from the safety of Max's embrace, as the man cornered something at the end of the hallway. He bent at the waist and scooped it up and an angry yowling sound filled the air.

He spun and looked at us apologetically. "I'm sorry. My girlfriend's cat got out and while I think he's a pain in the ass, she loves it."

The pain in the ass cat seemed offended and began swishing its tail back and forth, slapping his jailor's thigh with the white-tipped end.

I let out a little relieved laugh and straightened, pulling away from Max and his incredible warmth (Had he always been this warm?). "It's no problem."

The man started to smile, but it was short lived because behind me, Max wasn't as forgiving. "Watch where you're going next time," he said, short. "She could've been hurt."

"I'm sorry," the man said again, hurrying back down the hall, giving us a wide berth. I glanced at Max, shocked that he would even say anything, and became even more shocked that he was glaring at the man as he and his cat hurried to the threshold of their apartment. Before going inside, he glanced back to give me an apologetic look, but when he caught Max's stare, he rushed inside and shut the door.

I swung around to ask Max what his problem was, but before I could ask, I stumbled again, forgetting that the heel on my shoe was broken.

Max caught me by the elbow, steadying me.

"I broke my shoe," I said, then wondered why I was stating the obvious.

"I see." The corner of his mouth picked up.

We looked at one another for long seconds before he released me to push the door open again. "I'll wait while you change them."

Inside the apartment, I took a steadying breath. I wasn't sure what was wrong with me tonight. I was so jumpy and scared.

Of course, that isn't what bothered me most, because those things could be explained away after last night.

What bothered me more than anything was my reaction every single time Max touched me.

I didn't want to admit it.

But I couldn't ignore what my body was blatantly saying. In the entire year Max and I were a couple, his touch never, not one time, erupted such a flurry of butterflies within me.

Until now.

The lawyer in me was perplexed by this. My inner logic told me it wasn't possible. Yet the evidence was swirling around inside me with every erratic beat of my heart.

It left me with one resounding question.

Why?

9

Tucker

Consciousness came to me slowly, like the way a roasting fire spread warmth on a cold winter's day. It creeped over my skin, bringing awareness to my sleep-induced world.

The first thing I noticed was the weight against my side, the feel of something wrapped around me. Automatically, I shifted closer; the feeling of her skin was just so damn appealing.

I felt like my body was supporting her weight, like she had wrapped herself around me and I was her mattress. She was still and warm. The length of her arm wound around my middle with the tips of her fingers tucked between me and the sheets, as if her fingers didn't want me to touch anything but her.

Her cheek was pressed against my pec, her breath fanned out over my T-shirt, and for a fleeting minute I wished my chest were bare so I could feel the full effect of her against me.

My fingers twitched, and it was then that I realized my arm was wrapped around her middle, my hand was draped across her belly, and her belly was bare.

My fingers twitched again.

My already hard cock jerked beneath the sheets with anticipation. I never did morning sex with one-night stands… but I could make an exception just this once.

My cock jumped again and I groaned. The need to bury myself in something moist and warm was slightly overwhelming. Damn, last night hadn't sated me at all.

She shifted in her sleep, her thigh hooking over my legs and resting there. I began to draw slow, deliberate circles over the bare skin of her waist. Inching closer as I moved to the waistband of her pajamas…

My eyes snapped open.

Pajamas.

I was not in bed with some one-night stand.

I was in bed with Charlotte.

I froze, wondering what the hell I had been thinking. My God, if I hadn't realized what I was doing, I likely would have started fingering her!

What the hell was she doing draped all over me like a blanket? When we went to bed last night, I made sure to stay way over on my side of the bed. Away from her. At first, I was worried she might think that was odd, but she didn't seem to think it was strange at all. 'Course, I should have realized that her and my brother probably didn't get it on every night when she came to bed wearing those ridiculous satin pajamas.

Pants and a shirt.

Did she really sleep like that all the time?

Yep. And judging from the inside of Max's drawers, so did he. What the hell was this, *Leave it to Beaver?*

The thought of wearing a long-sleeved satin shirt to bed made me want to turn in my man card to the first man I saw, so I compromised by wearing the pants (Thank God they were blue; I would have drawn the line at some damn girly color) and a white T-shirt.

If Charlotte noticed the change in my nightwear, she hadn't said. Which means she probably hadn't noticed. She didn't miss anything.

And she was definitely a lawyer.

I learned that at dinner last night… along with a bunch of other useless information.

Some of the things I learned are as follows:

1) Max drank red wine with dinner. (I was having beer withdrawals.)
2) Max and Charlotte hadn't been out to dinner together in months.
3) They were both workaholics.
4) Her hair looked stupid in a bun
5) She didn't know where the flash drive was.

So much for using last night's meal as my first round of investigation.

As far as I could tell, she knew nothing about a flash drive. She didn't even seem to realize Max was having trouble at work (Trouble being his co-workers wanted to kill him).

Frankly, I was ready to write her off as no one useful at all, but something held me back from that.

Because amid all the useless information and boring dinner conversation, I picked up on something. Something that had me interested.

Charlotte was jumpy. The way her eyes would scan the restaurant, the street, the hallways in the apartment building… it told me that she was afraid of something.

But what?

I thought about coming right out and asking her, but I wasn't sure if I should.

She kind of acted like she didn't want me to see her fear.

Oh, Charlotte, what is going on in that pretty head of yours? My hand moved with the thought, gently brushing over her hair, my fingers tangling a little in the soft strands.

I froze.

I didn't stroke women's hair.

Ever.

The action must have seemed foreign to her as well because she woke immediately and, judging from the way her body tensed, our little sleeping position was not a regular kind of thing.

Was she frigid or something?

Wearing her hair in a tight bun at the base of her neck, a black suit, and pumps to dinner and a pajama set to bed… maybe she was lousy in bed. Maybe she was one of those women who hated sex. Maybe my brother had been miserable in this relationship and was looking for a way out.

An image of her red toenails flashed into my mind.

Frigid women didn't pain their toes red.

Did they?

She tilted her head back, her cheek brushing over my pectoral muscle, causing my nipple to harden into a firm pebble. There was a little bit of surprise in her eyes. "Morning," she said, her voice husky from sleep.

"Hey," I murmured, my fingers spasming on her waist. She bit back a gasp.

It gave me an idea. A fun one.

I was going to find out if women with red-painted toes could be frigid or not.

I stroked the area of her waist that was bare, just below where her shirt had ridden up. Her skin was smooth and warm, soft to the touch, and I stroked it again. She watched me with a wide stare, not looking away, as I grew bolder, dipping my fingers downward, brushing over the hip bone that jutted out softly and down, caressing over the soft flesh of her belly and drawing a circle around her belly button.

I heard her swallow, a thick movement, along with a soft intake of breath.

I was affecting her.

Inching just a little farther south, I played with the waistband of her satin pants, slipping just beneath them, like I was thinking—like I was planning… on going lower.

I felt the beat of her heart against my side. It was racing, thumping heavily in her chest. Leaving my fingers just inside her pants, I glanced at her. I caught her hazel stare with mine and a small wave of tenderness filled me.

It was a feeling I wasn't really used to and I shut my eyes against it. But even as they closed, I could still feel her. I could feel the satin of her skin, the pounding of her heart. Without thought, I leaned down, placing my lips against her hairline, breathing in that fresh and calming scent.

I allowed my mouth to linger, to graze her forehead as I pulled back. Her hand tightened on my waist and then began to move, sliding upward toward my chest and settling right above my heart. Her fingers twisted in the soft cotton of the shirt, and I swear it was like an open invitation to her waiting lips.

I RSVP'd to that invitation instantly.

Moving swiftly, I rolled over her, pinning her body into the mattress, and swooped down, claiming her mouth with mine.

An electric jolt of satisfaction cracked through me like a lightning bolt in a storm. I increased the pressure, pushing us together even closer, taking in the feel of that heart-shaped mouth, rubbing my lips over hers, creating a delicious friction between us.

She groaned lightly and I swept my tongue insider her mouth, slipping past her teeth and brushing against the roof of her mouth. The palm of her hand flattened against my shoulder, pulling me even closer.

I kissed her, our lips melding together, and I didn't break contact—not even for a second. It was as if our lips were two magnets that couldn't stand the pull another second.

My hips moved of their own accord, surging forward, rocking against her core. I was so hard that it was almost painful. My body cried out for release, and in that moment, I could only think of one thing: burying myself so deep in her body and pounding away until I poured every last ounce of desire out of me and into her.

Below me, Charlotte gasped, breaking our lips apart and staring up into my eyes. Her breathing was heavy and with every indrawn breath, her chest would push against mine. The desire in her eyes was undeniable. All thoughts of this woman being frigid completely vanished and raw hunger took over.

On my way to capture her lips, a loud beeping broke through the moment.

"Oh!" she said, wiggling out from beneath me to roll over and hit a button on the alarm clock beside the bed.

I collapsed on the sheets and shoved my head into a pillow.

Sleeping with Charlotte was not in the plan.

Being turned on by Charlotte was not in the plan.

For once, I was going to have to keep it in my pants. How the hell was I going to keep it in my pants when it was straining to get out?

"Max?" a voice to my left asked softly. I felt her timid touch on my shoulder.

I flipped over, staring up at the ceiling. "What?" I asked gruffly.

"Never mind," she replied, withdrawing from me and the bed. Just before she slipped out completely, I rolled and caught her wrist.

"I'm not mad at you. It's the alarm I'm mad at." I was an ass before. Usually I wouldn't care, but I had to live with her for a little while longer and she didn't know it, but she'd been through enough already. Finding out my brother was dead was going to be enough for her to deal with.

I didn't want her to think she had done something wrong, something that made me not want her. The truth was if that alarm hadn't gone off, I would likely be deep in her right this moment. The realization made my teeth slam together. I couldn't remember the last time I wanted a woman so badly.

She glanced over her shoulder. Some of her hair had fallen out of that ridiculous bun she put it in yesterday and framed her face. "It's okay."

I thought about brushing the blond strands away so I could see her eyes better. I didn't. I didn't trust myself to touch her at all right now.

She got out of the bed and I watched her as she went to the wooden dresser and pulled out what looked like black pants and a spandex top. Definitely not clothes to go be a lawyer in. Glancing at the clock, I realized it was just six a.m.

I remembered the gym I saw on the first floor when I came in yesterday.

A workout sounded like a pretty good idea right now. If I couldn't have sex, I could run my tension off on the treadmill.

My thoughts stalled when she began unbuttoning her top. *I should look away.*

I should look away right now.

To hell with that. I wasn't looking away.

The last button slid free and the white satin of her top slid downward, over her arms. She wasn't wearing a bra. She was completely bare.

Her breasts were full and high. Creamy globes that rounded heavily off her small frame with dark-pink nipples that were currently puckered into little pebbles. When she bent slightly to pick up her top, they shifted forward, hanging just a bit, and I had the vision of capturing one of those perfect globes in my mouth and teasing that little pink rock with my tongue.

Oh, the sounds that I could make her moan.

Yeah, I needed a run. A very long run followed by an icy-cold shower.

She lifted her arms and pulled the gray top over her head and for a few moments I gaped at her naked torso without holding back. Her face was lost in the top and all I could see was all that creamy, perfect skin…

"Mind if I join you at the gym?" I said, hoping out of bed and forcing my eyes away from her.

She paused. "You're not going to work out at the office gym today?"

Shit. I made a face at the wall. Max usually worked out at the office. He slept at the office. Did he ever come home?

"I need to work through lunch." I lied. "Busy day."

"Oh. Sounds good, then."

After adjusting my junk (I swear that's all I do around here), I headed toward the closet. I made it two steps.

There at the end of the bed she was bent over, pulling off her pajamas and thrusting her panty-clad ass in my face.

Did this woman think I was a saint?

Didn't she know she had to keep the goods put away if she didn't want me to jump her?

She bent down a little farther, tugging the leggings over her feet. Her ass was heart-shaped like her mouth…

I cleared my throat and changed course and went into the bathroom. Only after I heard her out in the kitchen did I go back in the bedroom to find a pair of sweats to work out in.

She met me at the front door and extended a bottle of water to me, which I took. "Thanks."

I followed her down to the gym on the first floor, alternating my stare between her ass and that god-awful bun. Why would she punish her hair that way?

She had a nice body. It was clearly visible in the workout clothes and not hidden under some nun suit or baggy pajamas. As I watched her step on the stair climber, I realized that what I was seeing right now was likely the most dressed "down" she ever got.

Charlotte Rose Carter was a tense, no-nonsense workaholic. If my theory was right, she was probably a stickler for routine, never had any fun (which she proved at last night's snooze-worthy dinner), and never had sex.

No wonder my brother slept at work.

I glanced at her ass bouncing around as she worked out. Tearing my eyes away, I turned on the treadmill and began to warm up. When my eyes started to stray in her direction again, I cranked up the speed and started to run.

She sure acted like she never got any sex, and while I pitied my brother, I couldn't help but remember the way she reacted to my touch this morning when she was pinned beneath me. There was a fire inside Charlotte. It was buried beneath her stuffy clothes, lesbian-style hair, and proper demeanor.

It made me wonder if Max ever bothered to dig deep enough to find it.

10

Charlotte

I couldn't concentrate. It didn't matter how many coffees I consumed or how many ice waters I drank. I opened the window in my office to let in the brisk air. I played annoying, fast-paced rock music in the background while I went over depositions.

Nothing worked.

My mind replayed this morning over and over again.

My body relived the sensation of Max's fingertips against my skin. The sensation of goose bumps rising across my flesh when his lips brushed my hairline was a reoccurring echo across my body.

My clothes felt tight. My skin too warm. And I was hungry. But nothing I ate or tried to eat was appetizing.

Never had he ever made me feel this way. *No one* had ever made me feel this way.

Was this desire?

Was this what all the girls in the office stood around the water cooler on Monday morning's giggling about?

I thought I knew desire. I thought I understood the pull between a man and a woman.

I didn't know anything.

Before packing up the documents I would need later this evening, I reconfirmed with my clients the dinner meeting was still on. It was and so I gathered everything I would need and started walking home.

My office was several blocks away from our apartment, but it was still a manageable walk. When the weather was bad, I usually just took a cab, but otherwise, I liked to walk, even if it was cold.

A lot of days my walk to and from work was my quiet time. My time to decompress between work, social obligations, exercise… It was my time to just be.

I wasn't sure what it said about me that my "quiet" time took place on the crowded and loud streets of New York City, and it was the one thing I didn't try to analyze. Probably because I was afraid of the answer I might conclude.

Today my quiet time was intruded upon.

Not by thoughts of my work meeting tonight.

Not by memories of my time in bed with Max this morning.

I was intruded upon by a feeling. A creepy feeling of being watched. This wasn't like that overused feeling from books and movies. This wasn't the hair rising on the back of my neck, the *stop and look behind you to see nothing at all* feeling.

It was an awareness. The kind of awareness that felt like a cold wind brushing over your skin. A pit of dread that settled in your gut and left you waiting. Waiting for something bad to happen.

I didn't bother to look behind me. Like I said, no one would be there. For all I knew, this was just another side effect from the other night.

Was it possible to have PTSD from attempted kidnapping? That seemed rather dramatic and I was not a dramatic type of person.

I was sensible. I was smart.

I stopped walking and hailed a cab.

I rode the rest of the way home in silence. But it was not quiet.

My mind was filled with more thoughts than usual. Like someone poured everything in my brain and shook it up. Usually my brain was like a filing cabinet. Neat and orderly. I thought of Max and his lips. I thought about the talking points I came up with for dinner. I thought about what I should wear to dinner. I thought of Max and the way he looked in that leather jacket last night. I thought about that creepy feeling I had and wondered if it was safe to go into my apartment and be alone.

By the time I pulled up to the building, paid the driver, and trudged inside I didn't really care if there was an army of angry bears in my home. I was pissed, frustrated, and mildly frightened. If anyone was waiting upstairs for me, I would clobber them with my briefcase and call the cops.

I knew Max wouldn't be home—it was still too early—but I anticipated seeing him again. I wondered if he would give me that fluttery feeling inside. I wondered if he would touch me… and what the effect of that touch would be.

I barely noticed the little note stuck to the front door as I unlocked it and let myself inside.

It was white and yellow with the words "first attempt" circled on the side. I rolled my eyes and snatched it off the door before I shut it and threw the lock.

"Mom," I groaned out loud. "How many times have I told you to send me stuff at work?"

I might as well just stop telling her; she wasn't going to listen. She didn't understand the amount of hours I worked. The fact that I was never home when the UPS guy came by with deliveries and then had to trek to the UPS store to claim my package was something she would never grasp.

I giggled on my way to the bedroom. She probably did it on purpose. It was her own way of making me leave work early at least once in a while to get to the post office before they closed.

"Well played, Mom," I said to no one. "Well played."

I jammed the UPS claim ticket in my purse and tossed it on the bed. I didn't feel like showering again today so instead, I changed into a black pencil skirt and jacket and reapplied my makeup so it looked fresh. The bun I styled my hair in was still in place so I didn't bother to restyle it.

I looked professional. I looked like a woman to be taken seriously.

I pulled out my notes to go over before the meeting. Knowing general personal details and such always helped close a deal because it showed that the firm did their homework and was thorough.

The whole time I read, my eyes would stray to the front door. I kept wondering about Max, about what time he would be home tonight.

I wanted to see him again. I couldn't put my finger on it, but something was different about Max, something had changed. Not only that, but there was a tension between us that I never felt before. When we were together, the air in the room seemed hotter, seemed to crackle.

I felt the blood drain from my face.

Was he angry at me?

Had I done something wrong without realizing it? Was Max thinking of ending our relationship?

That would explain his gruff demeanor, his delayed replies when I asked him a question. And when he did speak, he was sometimes so vague that it was like I was having a conversation with someone else completely. Max had never been vague. He was straight to the point. He hated wasting time on details that didn't matter.

And the way he kissed me this morning…

His lips seared me to my very core. He'd never kissed me like that before.

Even on a Saturday.

Maybe it wasn't desire I'd been feeling. Maybe the heat, that spark, was anger.

Maybe there was someone else. Maybe Max had fallen madly in love with another woman and just didn't know how to tell me.

I packed up my notes and smoothed out my clothes. My stomach felt queasy. Yeah, Max and I never had a great romance or epic courtship. Neither of us had time for dates, lazy days, or weekend trips. This wasn't a movie. This was real life and we both had lofty career goals. We both knew what we wanted.

It was only natural that two up-and-coming professionals in the New York City corporate world would be a perfect match. His connections became my connections and mine his. Everyone always said what a perfect pair we made when we were out at events and corporate dinners.

I thought he was happy.

I thought I was happy.

I barely noticed the cold when I stepped out onto the sidewalk and raised my arm to hail a cab. My swirling thoughts were far more chilling than the wind could ever be.

If I was so happy, then why on Earth did the idea of Max ending our relationship *not* reduce me to a pile of tears?

11

Tucker

The tall building was all glass and steel, standing over the sidewalk and busy street like some kind of castle among peasants.

It didn't make me feel inferior; if anything, it pissed me off.

This was the building where my brother found his demise. This was the building that in some aspects ultimately claimed his life. Yeah, okay, so buildings couldn't kill people... but the things that went on within walls of buildings certainly could.

The dress shirt and tie around my neck felt like a noose, and I rolled my shoulders back, trying to shrug off the feeling and the thoughts of my brother's death. I wished I could walk in there and smash some heads and bust some jaws... but I couldn't.

Yeah, it would be satisfying, but it wouldn't help me get Max's killer.

I tilted my head and glanced at the building once more, seeing it in a new light.

Max's killer was inside.

I stepped up to the wide glass doors leading in from the sidewalk and as I did, it swung open, a doorman appearing in a pressed suit and a smile.

"Good morning, Mr. Patton!"

I wasn't used to being called Mr. Patton. I was used to just Patton. But he wasn't talking to me. He was talking to Max.

"Morning," I said, inclining my chin. "Have a good day."

"You too!" the doorman called after me as I pressed the button for the elevator to take me to the twelfth floor. Unfortunately, I wasn't the only one in the car on the way up, but no one spoke as we all rode up in silence, making several stops along the way.

When we reached my floor, the doors slid open silently and I stepped out in the reception room of the office onto a buffed, light-colored tile floor and cream-painted walls. The reception desk was large and took up a huge amount of floor space, and as I walked, a dark-headed receptionist in a bright-red suit looked up.

She did a double take.

"Mr. Patton!" she said, standing up, her dark hair falling over her shoulders.

"Morning," I said, gripping my briefcase a little tighter. I hoped she didn't expect small talk because I planned to make a beeline for my office and shut myself in. I did not want to deal with anyone that I didn't have to. The less I talked, the easier being Max would be.

The receptionist watched me with this odd look on her face and I started to feel little tingles of warning. Was she not expecting me today? Because if she wasn't, then that meant she was in on the plot to kill Max.

"Is something wrong?" I asked coolly, glancing around for some sort of name tag or desk plate. I didn't see one.

"No—I…" she stuttered and I stopped walking toward the hall that I knew led to Max's office and turned to look at her directly.

"That didn't sound very confident."

She fidgeted in her chair. "I just didn't expect to see you…" Her voice faded away.

"Why?" I asked point blank.

"Because…" She began wetting her lips with her tongue. "They told me you weren't coming back. They're cleaning out your office."

Motherfuckers.

I felt my eyes narrow and anger darken my vision. Those assholes had no clue who they were dealing with. "Are they?" I asked, my tone taking on a dead calm. "I hadn't realized I'd been fired."

The girl looked at me with a mixture of sympathy and alarm in her eyes.

"I'll go find out what's going on right now."

She didn't try to stop me as I strode down the hallway, passing offices and cubicles as I went. Several people called out greetings and I returned them, but as I drew closer to where I knew my office to be, I started getting mixed looks. Looks of surprise. Looks of confusion.

If I had any doubt that someone in this company killed my brother, I sure as hell didn't anymore.

I wondered what these people had been told when he didn't show up yesterday, and now someone was in his office, clearing out all his stuff.

The thought made my heart begin to pump furiously. They were probably searching his office, looking for that flash drive.

I had to find it first.

Quickening my steps, I approached the small office that Max occupied. The door was slightly ajar and inside I could hear someone rifling through papers and opening desk drawers.

I laid my palm on the front of the wooden door—the door that still had Max's name on it—and pushed it open.

The man standing behind my desk looked up in irritation.

The irritation quickly vanished and I was very pleased to see blatant shock ripple through his entire body.

I knew then that this bastard had a hand in murdering my brother.

Red spots that looked suspiciously like blood swam before my eyes, blocking a lot of my vision and making me think of causing him serious pain. I'd never hated someone just on sight until now. Even if he hadn't given such an obvious look of guilt, I would have hated him.

He looked smarmy. He looked dirty. He looked like a corrupt businessman that cared about no one but himself.

It was going to be an absolute pleasure to make this asshole suffer.

I cocked my head to the side and did a sweeping glance at the box on my desk, the messed-up papers, and the guilty look written across his ugly face. "Did someone forget to tell me I was fired?"

"Maxwell," the man said, casually pulling his hand out of the drawer he had been searching. He gave a nervous laugh and then glanced at the door— the door which I was blocking. He glanced back at me, plastering a fake smile across his face. The little beads of sweat that gathered at his hairline gave me an immense amount of pleasure.

"Who said you were fired?"

"Well, the receptionist sure seemed surprised to see me. Along with several other employees. Why else would you be going through my desk and boxing up my belongings?"

He cleared his throat. "You certainly are not fired!" He tried to laugh. It sounded more like he was being strangled. "We became worried yesterday when you didn't come into work. We tried to call, but you weren't answering. We were very afraid something was wrong."

"So you automatically come in here to box up my stuff?"

"I just didn't want anything to happen to your items while we were figuring out where you were."

What a lying sack of shit. I sincerely wanted to plow my knuckles into his garbage spewing mouth. This son of a bitch thought my brother was dead.

I took a breath, reigning in my extreme temper. "So I'm not fired?"

"Of course not! We would never fire one of the most bright, young, and promising men at this firm."

Uh-huh.

And mother's liked watching their sons go off to war.

"What happened yesterday? It's not like you to not show up. To not call. Is something wrong? Is Charlotte okay?"

My back teeth slammed together. I did not like hearing Charlotte's name on this scum's lips.

"Charlotte is fine," I said, short. "I had a bit of an accident."

"Oh?" he said. The sweat on his forehead was much more pronounced now.

"Someone ran my car off the road," I said, watching him very carefully.

His eyes widened and his lips parted. It was a good impression of being surprised. "My God! You weren't hurt?"

"No, but my car was totaled. It was quite a mess to clean up," I said, flat. "And my phone was destroyed so I couldn't call in. I'm sure you'll understand." I looked directly into his eyes, not backing down, not so much as glancing away.

"Of course, of course." He came around the desk and motioned to my office. "So glad you're okay."

I almost laughed. I considered picking up the stapler on the end of the desk and hitting him upside the head with it. I considered confronting him here and now about his dirty, underhanded dealings.

But I didn't.

I needed to control myself.

Self-control wasn't something I was good at.

"Was there something you needed?" I said, changing the subject abruptly. I wanted to keep him on his toes.

"Excuse me?"

"You were going through my desk. Is there something that you needed? A file? A phone number?" *A flash drive.*

"Oh, yes," he said, his eyes darting around. "I was looking for the Matthews account file."

"It was likely in my car the other night. Nothing was salvageable."

His face paled. "You're very lucky to have not been hurt."

"Oh, I don't know about luck," I said, walking around and taking a seat in the black chair behind my desk. After getting comfortable, I glanced up. "I'd call it more divine intervention."

"You would?"

"It's not my time to die. There are still some things here on Earth that I need to do." I enjoyed the ominous undertone to my words. I hoped he understood exactly what I was saying.

I'm coming for you, fucker.

"Well, we're certainly glad to have you back, Maxwell," he said, turning to leave.

"Mr. Wallace," I called and he turned back. Thank God the Feds made me learn some of the names of people who worked here (or rather the suspects).

"I'll get another copy of that file you were looking for and get that over to you ASAP."

"The file?" he said, like he had no clue what I was talking about.

"The Matthews file?" I said like it was obvious. *Idiot.*

"Oh, yes. Please get that to me. I need it right away."

"I'll just get the info off my flash drive here and print it out." I patted my briefcase as he walked away.

My words halted his steps.

He turned to look at me.

"What did you say?"

"I said the information you were looking for is on my flash drive."

Our eyes locked.

In the moments that passed, we both knew exactly what we were talking about.

"You son of a bitch," he breathed out.

I smiled.

It was a real smile. The smile of a predator. "Something wrong, Mr. Wallace?" I asked innocently.

His face flushed and he took a step forward. I couldn't wait to hear the threat he was about to let loose. It made me wish I was wearing a wire.

Before he could speak, someone walked into my office behind him. It was a man of about sixty with gray hair and a crisp suit.

"What's going on—" His words halted.

He looked at me.

He looked at Mr. Wallace. His son.

Mr. Wallace Sr. was the driving force behind this company. He had been at the helm for almost thirty years. In the past five years, his son, Johnathan Wallace (the little puke I wanted to punch), had come aboard and that's when the money laundering, the fraud, and the espionage began to take place. Or so the FBI told me.

Looking at the two lizards now, I would surmise the Feds were right.

"Maxwell," Wallace Sr. said, "we were concerned about you."

I smiled and leaned back in my seat. "I was just telling your son here that everything was fine."

Wallace Sr. looked at Wallace Jr. They exchanged a silent word.

"Wonderful!" Wallace Sr. said.

"If either of you need anything I'll be in my office all day, catching up."

"Well, then." Wallace Sr. began. "Have a great day."

I watched them leave the room and then got up to shut my office door. Before I did, I watched the two men walk into a large corner office and shut the door.

I smiled.

They were likely calling up their hit men right now and demanding to know why I was still breathing.

I chuckled and shut the door to my tiny office. The walls were bare and it was literally shaped like a box. It made me feel claustrophobic. I couldn't understand how Max spent so much time in here.

I didn't have to understand. I just had to do what I came here to do.

Judging from the look on Wallace Jr.'s face, he hadn't found the flash drive. Which meant I still had time to get to it first.

I yanked off the navy suit jacket and tossed it on a nearby chair. Then I rolled up the sleeves of my white dress shirt and got to searching.

12

Charlotte

The hours in today seemed endless. As if this were some twisted form of *Groundhog Day* and I was doomed to live this day for all eternity.

Or maybe I just needed to take off these stupid heels.

Heels were like acceptable modern day torture for women. What was worse is that women everywhere actually *paid* for it. But nothing quite complimented a pair of legs like a hot pair of heels.

It was dark and I was exhausted so I hailed a cab once I left the restaurant and sank into the back of the yellow car, trying to ignore the pungent smell of onions. My stomach lurched. It reminded me of the man in my apartment.

The cabbie took off, veering wildly down the street and swerving around some walking bystanders who started yelling at his insane driving. I didn't even blink. All the cabbies in NYC drove like this. I used to pray every time I got in the back of one. Now I barely noticed. One time my driver actually hit a pedestrian on a bike. He didn't stop. In fact, he started muttering in some language I couldn't understand.

My business dinner could be categorized as a success. The clients would be coming by the offices tomorrow to sign the final papers. I already emailed the partners and their assistants so they could ready the paperwork so all it needed was some signatures.

They were going to be pleased. This was a big account, the biggest I closed. I was hoping they would let me sit in on the meeting tomorrow. After all, I was the one who did the legwork to get them to sign. It was my right to be there for the good part.

Pretty soon I was going to be handling cases and hopefully someday a partner. All those advanced early classes in high school, all those extra credits and heavy course load I took in college… all of it was for this. My father would be proud. I wished he were here for me to call and tell him about tonight.

I gazed through the window up at the sky and sighed. All the buildings and lights in the city made it almost impossible to see the stars. Sometimes I felt like if I could only see the stars, I might feel closer to my father… I might get a greater sense that he was watching me and that he approved.

My apartment building came into sight and I breathed out a sigh of relief. A glass of wine sounded really good right about now. After dealing with clients for two hours, I might need more than one.

The interior of the building was quiet and I enjoyed it as I waited for the elevator. Seconds ticked by (felt like hours), and I heard the telltale ding of the car as it slid into place and the doors opened.

I came face to face with Max and stepped back in surprise. "Max!" I said, and my insides began to tremble. His dark eyes swept over me, unreadable but intense. We stared at each other so long that the doors began to close and my heart skipped a beat because I wasn't ready to be separated from him yet.

Before that could happen, his hand shot out, stopping the doors from closing completely and pushing them back open to step out, bringing his body close to mine. Little shivers worked their way up my spine when his body heat enveloped me.

"Are you wearing new cologne?" I blurted when I inhaled. His scent was more masculine than usual. It tantalized my senses and caused something inside me to loosen.

The corner of his lip lifted with what looked like veiled amusement. "Yeah."

"I like it."

"Glad you approve." His voice was low and he crowded my space. Instead of stepping around me, he stayed right there, right on top of me, and once again little shivers climbed up my spine. It was delicious.

I cleared my throat. "You going back to work?"

He sighed like the idea exhausted him, and I looked up, tilting my head back so I could look up at his face.

"Actually, I was going out for a drink."

"A drink?" I wasn't sure I understood.

"Yeah. I feel like a beer."

"You drink beer?"

He made a face like he drank some sour milk. "Not usually. Tonight just feels like a beer night."

"Did you have a bad day at work?" I asked, a sinking feeling coming over me.

"It was fine," he replied, finally stepping back, putting a little distance between us.

So I was right.

He was trying to end the relationship. He was so unhappy he was going out to *drink beer* just so he didn't have to be around me.

Well, I certainly wasn't going to make him stay in a relationship he didn't want. I'd rather be alone. I wasn't going to wait for him to get up the courage to tell me he wanted out either. I was just going to tell him I knew what was wrong and then offer to move out.

Of course, before that happened we would have to come to sort of agreement about the lease, the rent, and the bills we shared.

"Earth to Charlotte," he was saying, waving a couple fingers in front of my face.

"What?" I said, coming out of my inner thoughts.

"I said you look like you could use a beer too."

I wrinkled my nose.

He made a rude sound. "Okay, a glass of wine," he amended.

"I was just thinking about having a glass." I admitted.

"Rough day?"

"Actually, I was able to close the account. I got the clients to sign!" It felt good to share my good news with someone.

"Rock on!" he said, giving me a grin. Then he held up his hand in between us.

I stared at it.

Did he want me to high-five him?

He did. He wanted me to give him a high-five.

I giggled and slapped my hand against his. When I pulled back, his fingers closed around mine.

"Come with me."

"To where?" I asked, breathless. How had I never noticed how fragile my hand felt in his before? And where had he gotten those calluses?

He shrugged and gave me a boyish grin. "First bar we come to."

I forgot all about how tired I was. I forgot about the pain my shoes were inflicting on my feet. All I could think about was the way my hand felt in his and the fact he wanted to take me out for beer.

"Okay," I said, suddenly excited about the impromptu date. This was the first time we'd ever done anything spontaneous.

He released my hand and grabbed my briefcase, taking over and tossing it behind a giant potted plant.

"What are you doing?" I demanded.

"Ditching the work. We can pick it up on the way in."

He threw my briefcase behind a plant. He wanted me to leave it there. I laughed. He didn't laugh with me. I gave him an incredulous look. "You're serious."

He lifted an eyebrow. "Do you really think someone is going to steal a briefcase full of legal documents?"

I opened my mouth to tell him that yes, that's what I thought. He didn't let me say anything, cutting me off to make a sound like he was snoring.

"Boring," he said.

I took a step to retrieve my manhandled briefcase. Max wrapped a hand around my elbow. "No you don't. Let's go."

He dragged me out onto the sidewalk. I was so surprised I couldn't even protest. He released me, looking up and down the street as if deciding where to go.

A cab drove by and he flagged him down, holding the door for me and climbing in behind me. "Take us to the closest bar," he told the driver.

"Have you hit your head recently?" I asked. If I wasn't so sensible, I might think aliens had invaded his body.

He didn't answer, which made me think he had hit his head. Then I thought of something else. "Where is your car?" I hadn't seen it parked on the street near the building lately.

He muttered something beneath his breath that sounded suspiciously like "freaking lawyer" before he turned to me to reply. "It's in the shop."

We were dropped off at a bar I'd never noticed before just a few blocks from our place. I was a little wary to go inside. I mean, what if it was unsafe? What if this was the kind of place that pedophiles congregated in to think about their next kidnapping.

I stopped walking.

What if the men who tried to kidnap me were inside?

"Charlotte?" Max said, turning to face me.

"This place could be full of criminals," I said.

He laughed. It was a deep laugh. "It's a piano bar."

"A piano bar?"

"Yeah, can't you hear the piano playing?"

Well, now that he mentioned it… "Criminals might like pianos." I pointed out.

"Is there an off switch for the lawyer in you?"

I felt my eyes widen. "Excuse me?"

"Come on, Charlie, you need a drink."

"Who the hell is Charlie?" I yelled as he dragged me toward the entrance.

"Charlotte," he corrected.

"Charlie is a boy name," I muttered as he paid the cover fee and we were waved inside.

Piano music filled the air, along with the deep tone of someone singing what sounded like an Elton John tune. The lighting was low in here, round tables scattered the room, and in the center was a giant wooden piano along with a small stage and various other instruments propped along the wall. People were laughing and singing along to the music. Waitresses weaved through the tables with trays full of drinks and chips.

"So what do you think?" Max said as he turned to me. "Are we gonna stay?" His smile was lopsided as he took my hand, waiting for me to give in.

The lawyer in me was ready to give a solid case of why we should leave.

The rest of me…

The rest of me wanted to stay.

He must have seen the look of surrender on my face because his smile turned smug as he towed me farther into the bar.

13

Tucker

I didn't find it. I searched Max's office endlessly. I looked in every possible place in the tiny space and came up empty.

And the phone.

His phone on the desk rang all day long. I stopped answering it after a while because I didn't have answers to any of the questions being thrown at me. I didn't understand his job or what he did. The corporate world was a long way from being an Armorer in the Marine Corps.

Don't get me wrong, I liked money. It would likely be nice to have a lot of it. But for someone who never really had a lot of it, I didn't understand why anyone would want to work with it and the people who had a ton of it all day long.

Money wasn't everything.

But clearly Max had been good at his job. His office was organized meticulously, his notes were thorough, and everyone in the office seemed to like and respect him.

Except of course for the Wallace men. It sure felt good to imply that I knew he tried to kill me and that I still had the drive he wanted. It was like plunging a knife in a terrorist and twisting it just a little to watch them squirm.

I'd done it once. I would do it again.

Of course, every time I would see one of them and the looks they cast in my general direction, I began to realize that while baiting Wallace Jr. felt good, it wasn't the smartest thing I'd ever done.

I pretty much painted a target on my back that screamed come and get me. They wanted me dead before and now they wanted it worse. They were going to come for me. It was just a matter of when.

I was going to be ready.

After I searched the office top to bottom and had enough of the damned ringing phone, I left. I didn't tell anyone I was leaving. I just walked out. I even left my office unlocked. Why not? What they wanted wasn't in there. I noticed a few gaping stares as I walked out, but I ignored them.

What were they going to do, fire me?

It was unlikely. They were going to want to keep me around so they could watch me.

I went the office gym and checked the locker that Max kept there (I told the attendant I lost my key so they cut the lock off and I bought a new one), but the only thing in the locker were gym clothes and a towel.

Next, I went to the bank to inquire about my safety deposit box, figuring Max had one. He didn't.

Frustrated, I went back to the apartment and searched it. It was tedious because I couldn't just toss things around. I had to be careful, not wanting

Charlotte to realize I'd been going through everything.

I spent the entire day sexually frustrated, irritated, and practically watching two assholes plot my murder. Oh, and I didn't find the damn drive.

I needed a beer. I needed several beers.

And then I ran into Charlotte.

She looked as exhausted as I felt. Even so, my cock hardened in my dress pants. I should have made up an excuse and left her there alone. I should have gotten the hell away from there fast.

But as I looked at her, I recalled when Wallace Jr. inquired about her safety. A fierce surge of protectiveness coursed through my veins. The thought of those bastards coming after her made my stomach sick. Men who hurt women deserved to rot in hell.

And I personally would escort them there.

I couldn't leave her alone tonight.

Next thing I knew, we were walking into a piano bar and I was teasing her about her name. Hell, it was a freaking miracle I even remembered her name.

I glanced at her across the round table. She was wearing one of those damn suits and had her hair pulled severely away from her face. Her wide hazel eyes roamed the bar; it was like she was seeing everything for the first time. She was timid, but deep down she was curious; that much was obvious. She had an inner wild child just waiting to be unleashed.

A waitress wearing a black spandex top and a pair of skintight jeans approached the table with a small tray in her hand. "What can I get ya?" she asked in her Jersey accent.

I ordered a longneck and Charlotte ordered a glass of red wine. Yeah, maybe I should have ordered something more Max-like, but goddammit, I needed a beer.

A few minutes later, the waitress returned and I grabbed the beer and took a long pull. Both women were watching me. It was like they'd never seen a guy drink before. "Keep 'em coming," I told the server.

Charlotte studied me over the rim of her glass. I knew her brain was working overtime and I wondered what the hell she could be coming up with now.

She set the glass down in front of her like it was some sort of shield. "Are you trying to break up with me?" she asked, point blank.

I choked on the beer I was in the process of drinking and yanked the bottle from my lips. A trickle of the beverage ran down my chin and I used the sleeve of the jacket to wipe it away. "What?" I said, incredulous.

"You've been acting weird. Sometimes it's like you're angry. Sometimes it's like you're a whole different person. And now we're here, in a bar, and you're chugging beer like it's liquid courage."

What would be the appropriate answer for this situation?

I drank more beer.

She leveled those green-flecked hazel eyes on me. "If you want out, say you want out."

I respected her approach. I was used to women who would try to sleep their way into a relationship, who would try to use sex to hang on to a man. Never had I ever once been with a woman who actually called me out on my behavior and gave me an out.

I set the beer on the tabletop with a thunk. "I don't want out."

"Then what the hell is going on with you?"

The waitress chose that moment to deliver another beer and glass of wine. I accepted it gratefully. "Better drink up," I told Charlotte.

"Are you having problems at work? Is that what this is about?"

"I don't really want to talk about it," I said, knowing those words would make her practically foam at the mouth for answers. It was my way of actually keeping the conversation going without having to give up information. I wanted her to give up what she knew.

"Max," she said, reaching across the table and taking one of my hands. An electric charge zapped through my body, like I was a completely dead battery that someone plugged in for a recharge. Sexual tension and desire threatened to take over my brain.

I used my free hand to deliver more beer into my system, hoping it would chill me out. The way she made me feel was unsettling. I didn't like it.

"You know you can talk to me. You mentioned before about some stuff going on at the firm. Is that still going on?"

So Max tried to talk to Charlotte about this?

"Yeah," I said, clearing my throat.

"Tell me what's going on. You know I can help you."

I made a face like I was doubtful and she shook her head and squeezed my fingers. "I know you said you didn't want me to get involved, but I'm involved already. I can see what this is doing to you. Maybe I can help. Maybe the partners at the practice can help you."

She leaned over the table toward me, her fresh scent wafting around me like some kind of scarf. "Do you need a lawyer, Max?"

So he hadn't told her anything. He was trying to protect her. If I hadn't already been feeling fiercely protective of her, then I would now. Knowing he wanted her kept safe was just more incentive to make sure no one hurt her.

"I don't need a lawyer," I said, leaning in so we were inches apart. "What I need is another beer and a night where we don't have to talk about this."

On cue, the waitress set another beer at my elbow on her way past. When I looked up, she gave me a wink. She was pretty hot.

Charlotte sighed and sat back, pulling her hand away to wrap it around her glass. We sat in silence for long minutes, listening to the piano player. I noticed she was drinking her wine faster now and it made me think of the way she looked when I first stepped out of the elevator.

"I'm not the only one who had a long day," I prompted.

"Yeah, but I scored a big client for the firm."

I tapped my bottle against her glass and we both took a drink. "'Grats," I told her, studying her features. "You know what I think?"

"What?"

"I think you don't like being a lawyer."

Her eyes flashed up to mine and she automatically started shaking her head. But I saw the truth when I first said it.

"You know how hard I've worked to be successful."

"But are you happy?" I asked, sitting forward, genuinely interested.

It was an invasive question, one it seemed Max never asked her, judging by the deer-in-headlights look I was getting. She gulped some wine, finishing off her first glass and reaching for the second.

"You ever had a beer?" I asked, hitching my chin at the bottle and changing the subject.

She wrinkled her nose. "You know I don't like beer."

"Have you ever tried it?"

"Ew." She sniffed haughtily.

I rolled my eyes. "So how can you say you don't like it if you've never tried it?" I pushed the amber-colored glass across the table toward her. "Try it."

She looked at me like I was insane. I did what I always did when a girl acted like she didn't want to do whatever it is I wanted her to do.

I put my elbows on the table and leaned forward, catching her eyes with mine and giving her a half smile. "Please?"

She swallowed thickly. It was clear I had an effect on her. She stared at me for long moments, our eyes not breaking contact. Then she reached for the bottle.

Watching those heart-shaped lips wrap around the rim had my stomach muscles clenching. I wanted her mouth around my dick.

Because my beer was otherwise occupied, I grabbed her wine and took a drink.

She timidly tilted the bottle up until the liquid spilled into her mouth and I imagined the distinct flavor spreading across her tongue and sliding effortlessly down her throat.

She tilted the bottle again and her eyes closed briefly, her golden lashes sweeping down to conceal what could be considered weapons in certain countries.

After a few moments, she held the bottle out to me. "I like it."

Her lips were shiny from the moisture of the bottle.

"Keep it," I drawled. "Watching you wrap your lips around that bottle is far more intoxicating than drinking out of it."

I heard her little gasp like it was the only sound in the room.

I signaled to the waitress that we needed more booze.

Charlotte took another sip out of the bottle and looked over at the piano. "This place is really cool. I like the piano."

People were throwing little scraps of paper into a giant glass fishbowl perched on the top of the piano, putting in requests for certain songs. Once a song would end, the man playing would reach in and grab one and then start playing again.

"Do you play?" I asked, forgetting it was likely something I was supposed to know.

She shook her head. "Always wanted to learn. Never had the time."

On impulse I reached out around the back of her head and found the damned clip that chained her hair back so fiercely, and I yanked it out.

"Hey," she said when I dropped the clip on the table between us.

Long hair tumbled down her back. It was wavy, probably from being twisted so tightly.

"I like it better down," I announced, picking up my newly delivered beer.

She ran her fingers through it, separating the waves and letting it fall over her shoulders and around her face. "You do?"

I nodded. "It suits you."

"I liked that leather jacket," she blurted. Then her cheeks turned scarlet.

A slow grin spread across my face. "Yeah?"

She nodded, giving all her attention to the beer and the piano man. I stripped off the suit jacket I was wearing and flung it over the back of the chair. Then I unbuttoned my sleeves and rolled them up past my elbows. I lost the tie hours ago. I hoped I never saw it again.

Charlotte's eyes wandered back to me, peeking through honey-colored hair. For a lawyer, she didn't have a very good poker face. Her desire was plain as day. How could a woman in a relationship be so hard-up for a good old-fashioned fuck?

"You never answered my question." I reminded her.

"Your question?"

"Are you happy?"

"I'm happy I've accomplished almost everything I set out to do. I like to think my father would have been happy too."

Oh shit. She had daddy issues. That explained a lot.

Ten to one, everything she did in life was to get the approval from some guy who didn't care. But she tried anyway, thinking some day he would realize everything he was missing.

"I wanted to call him today, after I closed the deal," she said softly, taking another sip of the beer. It was empty so I pushed another in front of her. "Sometimes I forget he's gone."

Gone as in died?

Well, shit.

"I'm sure wherever he is, Charlie, he's proud."

She glanced up when the nickname slipped out. I thought she might yell at me for calling her by a "boy name," but she just took another pull on the beer.

"Do you think they can see us? You know, from heaven?" Her voice was so small I had to lean forward to hear it over the music. I knew this wasn't a topic she brought up very often, and something in my chest expanded that she would trust me enough to talk to me.

She thinks you're Max. I reminded myself. I barely heard it though because she was laying into me with the full affect of those eyes. I threaded our fingers together. "Yeah. I think they can."

God, I hoped so. I thought of all the buddies we lost over in the sand that I wasn't going to forget. I wanted them to know that even though I lived, I wasn't going to take it for granted.

"Sometimes I wonder what my father would think of me, you know?" She leaned just a little bit closer and it was like everything else in the room ceased to exist. The piano, the bar noise, the drunk guy singing at the bar… it all went away. We were in our own little bubble, a bubble in which she completely captivated me and yet somehow made my heart beat just a little too fast.

"How long's it been, again?" I asked casually.

"Seven years." A faraway look entered her eyes. "I still remember the day of his heart attack like it was yesterday."

I gave her fingers a gentle squeeze. She glanced up. "Did I ever tell you I was the one who found him?"

A hard knot formed in the pit of my stomach. "No."

"He had come home in the middle of the day, maybe he left something in his office, and that's when he had a heart attack. No one was there to help him."

She paused for a moment and I gave her the time she needed.

"When I got home from school, he was there… lying in the living room, his hand just feet away from the phone. He was purple and so still."

"Don't," I told her. I knew what it was like to relive the vision of a dead body. To stare down at someone who was once full but was now completely devoid of life. I knew people sometimes turned bloated and blotchy looking when they lay for too long without anyone knowing they were there.

I remembered the smell, the vacancy in eyes that no longer saw.

"Max?" her concern broke through the fog of memories seeping into my mind.

"Yeah," I replied.

"You okay?"

"Of course." I looked at the beer at my elbow and thought about picking it up. But then I realized if I did, I would have to remove one of my hands from hers.

I wasn't that thirsty anyway.

"So…" I began, turning the conversation back to her. "Do they know what caused the heart attack?"

"Artery blockage. Stress. Lack of physical activity."

I had a feeling that was why she got up every morning at the crack of dawn to work out.

Her hair was so long that some of the strands falling over her shoulder dangled onto the table as she leaned close to me. It looked like bottled sunshine, even in this darkened piano bar.

I picked up a strand that was lying near our hands and rolled it around my fingertips, letting the softness wrap around my skin.

The air between us was charged, so much so that it practically vibrated my skin.

I wanted to kiss her. I wanted to press myself as close her as I could get.

A bright light turned on us and caused the moment to break. Both of us squinted and looked around for where the hell it was coming from.

The guy at the piano was holding a spotlight on us. A freaking spotlight.

His voice boomed over the microphone that was attached to the piano. "You know it's that time of the night for me to take a break and for someone out in the bar to entertain us all."

Seriously?

"And I couldn't help but notice the love birds sitting over there," he said, flickering the light on us once more. "So how about it? We need some entertainment!"

I glanced at Charlotte. Her eyes looked like saucers and she was shaking her head adamantly.

"Oh, no," she said, and I could tell she was ready to bolt.

I wasn't ready for her to leave.

I disengaged my hands from her and pushed back from the table. Everyone in the bar screamed and whooped.

Nothing like a bunch of drunk people to give a man confidence.

I heard Charlotte call my name and I shot her a grin, then walked toward the piano.

14

Charlotte

I was drinking beer.

In a piano bar.

On a weekday.

Not only that, but I was enjoying it. Like really enjoying it.

His presence was exciting, like being around him was somehow an adventure. And the way he looked at me… I'd never seen that look before. It was like I was a giant candy bar and he wanted to peel away the wrapper so he could inspect every inch of the chocolate.

It made me feel naked, yet I was fully clothed.

It also loosened my tongue.

Or maybe that had been the beer. Or the wine. Whatever it was, I just told him things that I only ever kept to myself. I never let anyone know how much I wondered about my father and what he would think of me now. I never talked to anyone about coming home from school that day and finding him lying dead on the carpet.

Those things affected me. Affected me in ways I still felt to this day. And I never spoke of them because it made me feel weak. It made me feel self-conscious.

But his touch acted like Miracle-Gro to a flower. I felt my petals, my feelings unfurling from deep inside me and opening up, blooming right in front of him.

And he didn't look at me like I was weak. He didn't look at me like my feelings were silly.

He looked like he understood.

How had we never had a conversation like this before?

I wondered what else we would have talked about had it not been for the piano man that, up until this moment, I actually enjoyed. Until he suggested I get up and sing, that is.

I did not sing.

As far as I knew, Max didn't either.

Did he?

I watched in fascination as he strode up toward the small stage. The navy dress pants hugged his butt a little more tightly than usual and his back muscles strained beneath the white dress shirt.

A few of the women sitting around whooped and whistled, and the burning sensation of jealousy scorched the back of my throat like acid. It was the first time I ever felt jealous that a woman was checking out Max.

Usually I found it flattering.

Tonight I found it annoying.

He stopped beside the piano and spoke briefly to the man who called him up there. He smiled and then crossed behind the large wooden instrument and bent, picking something up from against the wall.

Max draped a thick strap across his shoulder and swung a guitar up across his middle.

People in the audience cheered as he stepped across the stage and sat down, letting his feet hit the floor. A hush fell over the room. Even the singing drunk guy shut up (Thank God for that).

Anticipation coiled through the room like a deadly snake, and I found nerves fluttering around in my stomach for Max, wondering what in the world he was going to do.

And then he started playing.

His thick fingers strummed the chords on the guitar with perfection. A song I wasn't familiar with but he seemed to know with ease.

And then he started to sing.

The bottom dropped out of my stomach. His voice was absolutely stunning. Entrancing. Tunnel vision claimed me and it was as if I were staring through goggles that only pointed in one direction.

His.

His voice was raspy and jagged, like a broken piece of glass. There was so much emotion behind the words—which were about love and loss—that my heart began to ache. Every single person in the bar was completely ensnared.

I don't think anyone looked away; no one even dared to breathe.

My God, how had I lived with this man for almost a year and never seen him this way? Should I start stocking the fridge with beer?

The song dropped a little in tone and his voice slid down into that deep and smooth place that literally lifted the fine hairs off my arm. I hung on his every word.

He sang a line about never leaving and as he did, his eyes lifted, cut through the dimness shrouding the room, and looked at me. My heart skipped a beat. I lifted my hand toward my throat, my palm resting in the hollow place beneath my chin.

He watched me as his fingers moved. He strummed that guitar with such finesse and he didn't struggle, not one time. His voice kept perfect pace with the music… and then the piano started to play backup.

It didn't overpower his voice because he was so commanding that not even a bomb would do that. The music just accompanied him; it floated along behind him like the caress from a lover.

I wondered if his fingers would caress me like they did the guitar.

I squeezed my thighs together and squirmed a little in the wooden chair. He made me feel fidgety inside.

Then he closed his eyes, bowed his head, and delivered the last few lines of the song, his raspy, deep tone fading away with the music.

You could have heard a pin drop in the seconds that followed.

And then everyone erupted into mad applause. But I didn't. I still couldn't move. I still was wondering about this man—*feeling* him in ways I never expected.

My eyes caught on the way his hips swiveled as he weaved through the bar, back to our little two-person table. Even his movements seemed new to me, like I had been blind all this time, but now I could see.

It was so confusing.

Yet it was so achingly wonderful.

He lowered himself into the chair and gave me a little half smile, and I could have sworn I saw a little bit of insecurity in his eyes.

"I'm so sorry," I rasped, my voice literally scraping out of my throat.

His brows drew together. "What are you sorry for?"

I grabbed the bottle of beer and slid it closer to me, almost hugging it against my chest. "For never seeing you the way I see you right now."

The fleeting look that passed behind his eyes was of alarm and sadness. But it was gone so fast I couldn't ask him what it was all about.

"How do you see me right now, Charlie?" he asked.

"Real," I said, not knowing what else to say.

"What?"

"I just…" I began, tucking a strand of hair behind my ear. "I just always thought of you as this perfect guy. The guy who always knew what he wanted. The guy who never let emotion rule his head or his heart. The kind of guy who never stumbled a day in his life."

"And now?" Max whispered. I swear his face seemed paler than just seconds ago.

"Now I know I was wrong. There is no way anyone could have that kind of grit, that kind of soul in their voice, if they hadn't lived through pain. There's no way that kind of emotion can just be pulled out of thin air. You aren't perfect, are you,

Max?" I whispered the last part, sliding my hand across the table toward his.

He opened his fingers and mine slid into his palm, like it was exactly where they belonged.

"No. No, I'm definitely not perfect. I guess I'm not the guy you thought I was. I'm not the guy you wanted."

Why so much sadness in his tone?

"Can I tell you a secret?" The fluttery sensation in my stomach was so wild I felt like I was sitting at the top of a super steep roller coaster.

"Yeah."

"I like this guy better."

He jerked so forcefully his hand pulled away from mine and his chair slid back a couple inches. Then he snagged a bottle off the table and chugged the rest of it down.

"I gotta piss," he announced and shot up out of his seat and took off for the bathroom across the room.

I sat there and wondered what I said that was so wrong.

15

Tucker

My dick was broken.

It was so hard it was uncomfortable, and I couldn't leave the bathroom until it decided to knock it the hell off.

Okay, fine. My dick wasn't broken. Clearly, it was working just fine.

I needed to get laid.

Like STAT.

I should put Charlotte in a cab, send her packing, and then pick a girl—any girl—at the bar and go home with her. That would take care of this pecker problem.

I thought about a couple of the girls I noticed sitting at the bar. The blonde was pretty hot. An image of Charlotte flashed into my mind.

Okay, no blondes.

There was also a brunette. Brunettes were good.

I thought about Charlotte again. I heard the words she just admitted.

She liked me better than my brother.

Holy hell.

What a freaking clusterfuck.

I went over to the urinal and unbuttoned my jeans. Of course, he sprang out like some secret agent on a mission. Pissing with a hard-on wasn't the easiest task. It required some heavy leaning.

Stop thinking about your brother's woman, Patton! Think about someone else!

I thought back to the brunette at the bar. She had long, dark hair, pulled up in a bouncy ponytail. Her top was tight and her boots went all the way to her knees. She looked like the kind of girl I would take home any night of the week. She was exactly what I needed right now.

I looked down.

I wasn't hard anymore.

Apparently, thinking about my time tonight with the brunette wasn't appealing to my other brain.

With a sigh, I finished up in the bathroom and headed back toward the table. I realized that I never came up with a response in the bathroom. I had been too busy trying to slow my roll.

She probably expected me to tell her I loved her or some shit. I didn't tell women I loved them, even if that's what they wanted to hear. If I was gonna say it, I would damn well mean it.

All the more reason to put her shapely little ass in a cab.

When I arrived back at the table, Charlotte wasn't alone. She was accompanied by a tray of shot glasses, all of them filled with clear liquid.

Fury laced through me, like a match next to gasoline. What guy sent her over all these damn drinks? He probably saw me leave and was hoping to get her drunk and take advantage of her.

I'd beat his ass.

I began pushing up my sleeves a little more and dropped into my seat.

"Who sent these?" I demanded.

She seemed a little taken aback by my harsh tone, but I didn't care.

"It seems you have a fan club," she spat, her tone matching mine.

Wait, what? I glanced up for more of an explanation.

"Those girls over there sent them to you. Along with their regards," she said, flat.

I glanced over at the bar. Blondie and her dark-headed friend waved. I hitched my chin at them in thanks. They giggled and turned around.

"Ho bags," Charlotte muttered.

Beer sprayed all over the table when I began to choke. "What did you just say?" I asked in a strained voice.

She gave me a stare. "What self-respecting woman sends drinks to a man who is sitting with another woman?" she asked, her cheeks actually flushing.

I grinned. "Is someone jealous?"

She seemed to be very unhappy about that. She finished off her beer and stood up. Guess she wasn't jealous; she was pissed. She was probably leaving.

She wasn't leaving.

I watched as she unbuttoned the blazer she wore and slid it off her arms. Beneath it she was wearing a sleeveless, white silk top that had some kind of extra fabric around the neck that tied in a bow. It kinda looked like a scarf. Hell if I knew anything about women's fashion.

The shirt hugged her perky, round breasts and revealed a tight-fitting skirt that hugged her ass like a glove. She shook out her blond locks, tangling them around her shoulders, and then she leaned over the table, picked up one of the shots and saluted the girls at the bar.

The girls' eyes widened and Charlotte downed the shot in a single gulp. The empty shot glass made a heavy thud when she snapped it down on the tabletop.

As the alcohol pushed down her throat, she grimaced, screwing up her face like it was the first shot she'd ever had.

I couldn't help but laugh.

She sat back down and took a drink of my beer. "Did they see that?" she asked, eyes watering.

I glanced back at our audience. The girls were no longer looking. Charlotte made her point. "Nope."

"That's one thing about us lawyers," she said. "We don't like to lose."

Instead of replying, I downed one of the shots. Vodka.

We sat in silence for a few minutes, just drinking and listening to the music. I didn't look at her. I was afraid if I did, she would remember what we were talking about before I went to the bathroom. But her movements caught my attention and I turned to her. She was swaying to the music from her seat.

I looked at the table, littered with some empty bottles, shot glasses, and wine glasses.

"How much have you had to drink, Charlie?"

"A couple," she said, slumping slightly in her seat. She reached for a beer and I pulled it out of her reach.

"No more." I knew the look of a tipsy woman.

She stuck out her tongue at me.

"Better keep that thing in your mouth unless you plan on using it," I quipped before I could stop myself.

"Saturday is…"—she paused and counted on her fingers—"three days away."

"So?" I asked, wondering what kind of drunken conversation this was going to be.

She wagged her eyebrows at me.

I laughed.

The waitress came by and I asked her to bring some water for Charlotte.

"This was fun," she said, giving me a smile.

"Yeah?"

She nodded. "Your voice is amazing. I never knew you could sing like that."

"Thanks." Music was just a hobby. Something to pass the time when I was over in the sand. It was a way to deal with all the shit we saw over there. I hadn't really meant to start singing, but as soon as my fingers hit the chords on that guitar, it bubbled up out of me and I let it.

"I have to pee," she announced but didn't get up.

"You know that requires the bathroom, right?"

She giggled. "Duh. I'm not drunk."

"No, but you sure as hell are amusing."

She rolled her eyes. I liked seeing her like this. Relaxed. She stood and stepped around the table. Of course she wasn't watching where she was going and her foot caught on the leg of my chair and she stumbled.

Right into my lap.

She fit perfectly.

She squeaked and I wrapped my arms around her.

"These damn heels hurt my feet," she whined.

"Then why do you wear them?"

She lifted one of her long legs up into the air. "They make my legs look good."

"Yes, yes, they do," replied the man sitting behind our table.

My entire body tensed. I whipped around quickly, making Charlotte wrap her arms around my neck to keep balance.

"You looking at my woman's legs?" I asked, my voiced deadly calm.

He glanced at me. "Well, she was showin' 'em off."

"If you wanna keep your teeth, I suggest turning around."

Charlotte gasped. "Max!"

The guy turned around, muttering in his seat. I grabbed ahold of her thigh and pushed her leg down. "I know how nice your legs are, darlin', but no one else in here needs to."

She sighed and laid her cheek against my shoulder.

It felt nice.

What. The. Fuck.

What the hell was I doing right now? Calling her my woman. Calling her darlin'? Calling out some dude for checking her out…

I was losing my damn mind. What the hell was in that vodka? And now here she was sitting in my lap with her head on my shoulder and I was *enjoying* it.

"Weren't you going to the ladies' room?" I asked her.

"Oh, yeah."

I helped her up so she didn't fall on those shoes again and watched her make her way to the bathroom. I knew I was acting crazy, but even knowing it wasn't enough to not keep my eye on her as she went.

When the waitress came back around, I handed her some cash to settle up the bill and tip. The girls at the bar came sauntering over, and I wanted to groan. I had my hands full enough tonight with Charlotte. Usually I would welcome more than one woman's attention, but it seemed that Charlie required a lot more looking after than most.

"We liked your song," the brunette said, stopping beside my chair. She was pretty hot, with light-blue eyes and sleek, long hair.

"Thanks," I said, giving them a polite smile.

All thoughts of taking one of them home had vanished from my mind completely.

"Did your sister leave?" the blonde asked, and I had to give her props for her cleverness. Most guys would be leading them out of the bar already.

"I'm not his sister." A voice came from behind us.

I spun in my seat to see Charlotte standing there with her hands on her hips and her head cocked to the side. She didn't even look at me. Instead, she regarded the women with a cool, level stare.

"Well, you couldn't possibly be *with* him," the brunette responded.

"And why is that?"

Oh shit, this was going downhill fast. I stood up between the women. "Well, we gotta get going."

They ignored me.

"Because you don't exactly look like the type someone like him would date."

I was offended. For me and for Charlotte.

"Well, I guess he has better taste than skank," Charlie spat.

I stifled a laugh.

Then she started pulling off the heels she was just complaining about and brandishing one like a weapon.

Time to go.

I wrapped my arms around her waist and towed her up against my side. "Down, girl." After snatching our suit jackets off the chairs, I practically carried her out onto the sidewalk where the cold air greeted us.

"Put me down," she complained.

"Only if you promise not to clobber me with your shoe."

She laughed. "I promise."

I put her down, keeping my arm out just in case she stumbled.

"I'm not drunk," she said, giving me an evil look.

"Well, you sure as hell aren't sober."

"It's freezing out!"

"Put your shoe on." I reminded her dryly.

She put it on and fell over in the process. I rolled my eyes and bent down to pick her up off the pavement.

"Okay, maybe I'm a little tipsy." She allowed as I hauled her up.

"Ya think?"

She fell against my chest and her head fell back so she could look up into my face. "Did I tell you I liked your song?"

"Yeah." My eyes wandered down to her lips.

She watched me watch her. "You can, you know," she said softly.

The blood was pumping through my veins at an extraordinary speed. It felt like I had a jackhammer inside my body and it was creating all kinds of chaos.

I lowered my face a little bit more so our lips barely grazed one another. She sighed and her eyes drifted closed.

Maybe the perfect guy could resist such an action.

Charlotte already pointed out that I was not perfect.

I pulled her even farther against me, lifting her feet up off the pavement completely, and her hands came up to wrap around my biceps, holding tightly as my mouth staked its claim.

God, her mouth was sinful. And hot. Her kisses were a direct contrast to the wind blowing around us, and I wrapped my other arm around her, holding her firmly in place so my tongue could delve past her lips and explore the depths of her mouth.

She tasted like beer (my favorite) and I growled as I licked even farther into her mouth. Her tongue met mine and they twisted together as our lips smashed against one another, desperately trying to get closer.

Her deep inhale pressed her chest against me and even through our clothes I could feel her rock-hard nipples standing at attention. One of my hands slid down and cupped her luscious ass, tilting her body even closer. But it wasn't close enough. I wanted her legs wrapped around my waist. I wanted to feel the sleek moisture between her legs coat my abs and cock.

One of her hands slid up the back of my head, her fingers threading into my short hair and creating friction against my scalp.

Holy shit, I wanted to push up her skirt and do her right here on the sidewalk. I didn't even care who saw. Never in my life had my body demanded sex more.

She pulled her mouth away, gasping for breath, and her head fell forward so that her forehead rested against mine.

A little shiver started at her feet and shook her body. I pulled back, slowly sliding her down the front of my body. I knew she could feel the hard length of me; there was no hiding it.

"Here," I said, my voice sounding foreign to my own ears. I lifted up her blazer and held it out so she could slip her arms inside.

"Thanks," she said softly as I buttoned up the waist. When I was finished, my hands lingered a little bit longer than needed in the area just below her breasts.

"Come on," I said, draping an arm over her shoulder and tucking her against my side. We started walking as I kept my eye out for a cab.

It wasn't a far walk, but it was late and cold outside. Of course this would be the one night I didn't see any of the usual one dozen cabs flying dangerously over the streets. "Looks like we might have to walk the whole way."

"I don't mind. I like to walk. It's good for thinking."

"And what do you think about when you walk, Charlie?"

I felt her shrug under my arm and I didn't push. I already felt like I learned a lot about her tonight. Usually learning anything other than a woman's bra size was just too much information for me, but for some reason, Charlotte was different.

"Are you ever going to tell me what's going on with you?" she asked as we walked.

"Am I really that different lately?" I'm not sure why I wanted a play-by-play of how miserable at being Max I really was, but I guess I was a glutton for punishment. He always was the one that had his shit together.

"I've been worried."

"Don't worry," I told her. I wanted to add that everything was going to be okay, but I couldn't promise her that because things weren't okay right now.

Up the street I heard a car approaching and I turned to see a cab heading our way. I pulled away from Charlie to step up to the curb and hail it down.

Then all hell broke loose.

16

Charlotte

I loved watching him move. He had this way about him, this confidence that drew the eye. His shoulders seemed more square, his posture a little more straight. What's more, I loved the way he felt when he moved against me.

I thought I might die when he picked me up off the pavement, leaving my feet to dangle in the late-night air. I had been suspended. Suspended in moments of perfect bliss, where all I could feel was the hard contours of his body, his vise-like arms anchoring me against him, and the way his mouth felt moving over mine.

The erection in his pants had been mildly startling but completely alluring. Just feeling it press against my abdomen made my panties feel slick with moisture.

My body ached inside. It felt coiled with need. It begged for release as if it knew the next time Max and I were together, it would be far more satisfying than it had ever been.

I smiled to myself, all the alcohol I ingested making me feel relaxed and carefree. He stepped away from me, toward the curb to hail a cab. I stepped backward so I could lean up against the building. My shoulders hit the wall first, but it wasn't nearly as cold as I expected the contact to be. In fact, it didn't feel right at all.

I realized I hadn't backed into a wall.

But a man.

His arm snapped around my waist, roughly yanking me all the way against his body. I started to squeal, but the feeling of icy cold metal against the side of my head had me biting off any sound.

He had a gun. He was holding it to my head.

I was literally seconds away from a bullet plowing into my brain and ending my life.

Forever.

My eyes, already leaking tears, found Max where he stood at the street, his arm in the air. I wasn't ready to die.

"Give me your purse," the man demanded in my ear.

I whimpered and held it out.

Another man appeared in front of me. He too was holding a gun… He was also wearing a black ski mask.

He snatched the bag out of my hand, and over his shoulder, I saw Max begin to turn.

"Max, run!" I screamed, risking getting shot to warn him. As I yelled, I forced my body to go slack. The man holding the gun to my head cursed and grappled to hold on to my body as I dropped toward the ground.

I heard a shout and the pounding of feet, but I didn't see what was happening because the gunman grabbed a handful of my hair and yanked me back. He pulled so hard black spots appeared before my eyes. I cried out, unable to keep the sound of pain inside.

He jerked me so hard it kept me from hitting the ground. Instead, my knees hit the pavement, scraping over the rough concrete. As I knelt there, completely at his mercy, he forced the gun up under my chin, stabbing the delicate flesh on the underside.

"Come any closer and she'll be dead before you blink," the voice above me cautioned.

I forced my watering eyes open to focus on Max, who was standing just a couple feet away with a gun pointed directly at his chest by gunman number two. Instead of rifling through my purse, he was holding it like he didn't even care about it, dangling it over the ground without a second thought.

He kept his eyes on Max, while Max kept his eyes on me.

"Let her go. It's me you want," he said.

I know my hair was being pulled really hard, but I'm pretty sure my brain still worked and that sentence made no sense. They wanted our money, not him.

"Give me your wallet," gunman number two demanded of Max.

Max's eyes narrowed and flicked over to him. He didn't look scared. He looked pissed. He also made no move to grab his wallet.

"Give it to him!" the man holding me screamed and twisted his hand a little bit more. I bit my lip to keep from crying out. I looked at the ground, searching for something I might be able to use as a weapon.

This had to be the only street in New York that had spotless sidewalks.

Max looked at me again, trying to tell me something with his eyes. *Get ready to move.*

Then he glanced away. "I'm going to reach around to my back pocket and get my wallet," he said slowly. It seemed to take forever for his arm to finally reach around and find his back pocket.

"Hurry up!" the man holding me yelled and jammed the gun into my skin. I couldn't help it; I yelped. My skin burned with pain as tears filled my eyes. I waited for the popping sound of the gun. I waited for my life to end.

Max jerked his wallet out and extended it. Gunman number two reached for it, but Max had other ideas. Moving more quickly than I'd ever seen him move, he sprang into action, throwing the wallet at the man and knocking the gun out of his hand. It landed with a hard thunk on the pavement and Max kicked it, sending it skittering into the street and away from the man who was wielding it.

I watched as he quickly twisted the man's arm around his back so hard I heard his shoulder pop out of place. The man cried out and hunched over. Max was ready and brought his knee up, ramming it right into the masked face.

"Move!" he yelled at me.

I didn't think.

I twisted to the side, sinking my teeth into the meaty flesh of my assailant's thigh, and bit down.

So nasty.

Who knew where his thigh had been…

But a girl had to do what a girl had to do.

He screamed and I released my teeth, pushing up to run away.

I got two steps.

He hit me in the back, swinging the gun around and catching me right in the center. Pain exploded between my shoulders and I fell, landing on my hands and knees. I pushed up, but the man grabbed my ankle, causing me to fall back down, flat on my face. With him still holding my ankle, I spun, flipping over to see him (He was also wearing a mask) tower over me.

He grinned a maniacal grin beneath the black fabric and raised the gun. "You can't outrun a bullet."

Max plowed into him from behind, coming in low like some kind of out of control linebacker. He wrapped his arms around the man's waist and pushed off the pavement, ramming the gunman into the brick building.

The two men sprawled out on the sidewalk with Max on top. He drew back his fist and landed several solid punches before the gunman flipped them and pinned Max to the ground.

"Max!" I screamed as adrenaline pumped through my system. I couldn't even think. All I could do was feel as a flurry of emotion slammed into my body all at once.

It was almost paralyzing.

I couldn't think.

I had to think.

The gunman socked Max in the face and the sound of the pounding of flesh turned my stomach. I glanced around to see the other man lying unconscious on the ground, my purse beside him.

I ran to my bag and dumped the contents out on the concrete. Finding the only thing I thought might help, I ran back over toward the men, who were know grappling over the gun.

I ran over, holding up my weapon, ready to strike, when Max flipped the larger man off him and delivered a jab to his kidney. The man made a wheezing sound and Max grabbed the gun, twisting it around to take it away.

Our attacker was a persistent man, grabbing onto Max's wrist and pulling the gun back. Max leaned over as the two fought for control of the weapon.

The sound of a firing bullet cut through the night.

I screamed and closed the distance between us as both men collapsed, tangled in a heap, no longer wrestling.

The dark, unmistakable stain of blood creeped out from beneath them, winding across the pavement and pooling at my feet.

17

Tucker

I was a Marine (Yeah, I was out of the Corps now, but once a Marine, *always* a Marine). I had been trained in war. I had been trained to fight.

Didn't mean I enjoyed it.

But as I rolled off the asshole who shot himself while trying to shoot me and threatening to shoot Charlotte, I enjoyed seeing him bleed.

Fucker.

In fact, as I stood, I considered shooting him again.

"Max!" Charlotte screeched and plowed into me from behind. I spun, taking her weight and supporting it while planting my feet into the ground to keep us from falling over.

She pulled back, frantically searching my body, running her cool fingers all along my limbs and up my chest.

I'll be damned if my cock didn't start to respond.

Apparently he didn't care we were almost just killed.

"Where are you shot?" she asked, her words spilling over each other.

"Charlie," I said.

"Where's my phone?" she yelled. "I'll call 9-1-1!"

"Charlie—"

"Oh my God, you're bleeding. You're bleeding!" She gasped, placing her hands over the front of my white shirt, which was now saturated in red.

I caught her hands and squeezed. "I'm not bleeding."

"What?" she said, like my words weren't getting through to her.

I released her hands and grabbed her by the face, cupping her jaw in my palms and staring directly into her wild eyes. "Honey, listen. I'm not shot. That's not my blood. I'm fine."

"You're not shot?" she said, her voice wobbling.

"No." My hand skimmed down her neck to brush away some of the hair that was sticking to her tear-stained cheek.

A sob ripped from her throat as her arms thrust around me. Charlotte buried her face in my chest and cried. "I thought you were dead!" she wailed. "Dead!"

"I'm not dead."

"The blood…"

"It wasn't mine."

"They tried to rob us." She stiffened and pulled away. "They tried to rob us!"

Was it odd I thought it was cute the way she seemed to just remember we were in a deadly situation?

The man who shot himself (what a douche) groaned and pushed himself up to his knees. I turned, tucking Charlotte between me and the wall, my muscles tensing.

I reached down beside him and picked up the gun, cocking it and aiming it at his head. "You have shitty aim," I told him. "I don't."

"This was supposed to be easy." He moaned, pressing a hand to the bullet wound in his side.

I reached behind me and guided Charlotte's fingers into my belt loop. "Stay with me, sweetheart."

I moved along the wall, keeping the gun ready to fire as we made our way over to the guy who was laughingly easy to knock out. I kicked him. "Get up."

He didn't reply.

I kicked him again.

He jolted awake like someone threw cold water on him.

"Get your bleeding friend and get the hell out of my face."

His eyes widened when he saw who was in control now, and he leapt off the pavement, rushing over to his asshole friend. They started to move away.

"We have to call 9-1-1!" Charlotte whispered fiercely behind me.

I ignored her.

"Hey," I called out to Tweedle Dee and Tweedle Dum.

They looked up.

"You tell who sent you that if he wants me dead, he's going to have to try a hell of a lot harder than this."

The idiots grimaced.

For shits and giggles, I fired off a shot that ricocheted off the pavement just in front of their feet. They scattered like the cockroaches they were.

"They're getting away!" Charlotte yelled, rushing out from behind me and running after the men.

I grabbed her and hauled back into my side. "Let them go."

"Are you crazy?"

My eyes narrowed on her face. "You're bruised." Gently, I ran my thumb on the underside of her chin where a purple mark was already forming.

"So are you."

I took a hit to the face, a hit I wouldn't have taken at all if my damn reflexes hadn't been slowed down by the beer. No more drinking until this was over. "I've had worse."

She made a face. "You have?"

We bent to pick up her bag and scattered belongings. I made sure to look over everything, hoping to see a flash drive. There wasn't one.

I avoided her question. "You gonna be okay?"

"We need to call the police."

I took the phone out of her grip and stood, slipping it into my pocket.

"Give me my phone."

I stuck out my hip. "If you want it, go get it."

If looks could kill, I'd be dead.

I chuckled.

"How can you laugh at a time like this?" she demanded.

I sighed wearily. Because if I didn't laugh, I might lose it.

"No cops. Let's go."

Of course a cab chose that minute to show up. The last one abandoned us the minute he saw trouble brewing. If he saw the blood on my shirt when we approached the car, he didn't say.

We rode the short ride to the apartment in silence and then trudged into the building. I tucked the gun in the waistband of my pants and the weight of it was familiar and calming.

As I waited for the elevator, she retrieved her briefcase from behind the plant. Figured she would remember it was there. Upstairs, I unlocked the door and stepped in first, sure to keep my body angled to block Charlotte. I was half expecting someone to be lying in wait in the apartment, ready to finish what the idiots on the street couldn't.

It appeared to be empty.

But I wasn't about to let my guard down that easily.

I glanced at Charlotte over my shoulder and held a finger to my lips. Her face paled a bit, but she nodded and straightened her shoulders.

We made our way past the kitchen and stopped in front of the bathroom door. Pulling the gun out of my waistband, I pushed the door open and raised the gun.

The room was empty.

Keeping the gun out in front of me, I stepped into the bedroom. After checking the closets, I knew no one was here.

We were safe.

For now.

Charlotte collapsed on the end of the bed, tossing her heels on the floor and stretching out her bare toes. She looked exhausted and frightened.

"How are you handling all the alcohol you drank earlier?" I asked, wanting to make sure she wasn't going to spend the night praying to the porcelain gods.

She made a scoffing sound. "Whatever buzz I had going on was completely wiped out when someone put a gun to my head."

"What a waste of good alcohol." I sighed, shaking my head.

She smiled, but it faded away when her eyes zeroed in on the blood staining my shirt.

"I'm going to clean up a little," I said, leaving her and shutting myself in the bathroom.

I went to sink and glanced in the mirror. The flesh around my right eye was discolored and tender. I'd probably have a black eye come morning.

I stripped off the ruined shirt and tossed it in the garbage can. Afterward, I washed my hands and face at the sink and grabbed a towel to dry with.

After what happened today at the office and just now out on the street, things were going to go straight to hell fast.

I hated that Charlotte was mixed up in this. I didn't want to be responsible for her, for her safety. I didn't want her death on my conscience. It was heavy enough as it was.

The sound of the door being opened behind had me pulling the towel away from my face.

"Max, we really need to talk about what happened—" Charlotte was saying. And then her words halted.

She gasped.

I wasn't wearing a shirt.

I spun around, facing her, but by the look on her face, I knew that she had seen.

She started to speak and stopped. Her brow wrinkled and I watched as she struggled internally, wondering if she was seeing things.

I guess I should have locked the door.

Or maybe I hadn't because deep down I was hoping she would see.

"When did you get a tattoo?" she asked, her voice low and slightly off.

This was my moment to choose. I could make up some outrageous story and convince her it was true.

Or I could tell the truth about who I really was.

I like this guy better. I heard her words in the back of my mind.

The FBI told me not to tell her.

I didn't like to be told what to do.

I laid the towel beside the sink. "I got it several years ago."

"You got it *years* ago," she repeated, trying to make sense of what I said.

I nodded.

Her eyes swept over my bare chest, my arms, and then finally up to my face. Her lips parted, and I heard her indrawn breath.

"Charlotte, we need to talk."

She remained silent for long moments, then slowly she began to shake her head.

This was going to be harder than I thought. As I searched for the words, for the explanation I owed her, she turned and fled.

18

Charlotte

I knew.

All the odd little things he said, the leather jacket, the short hair. The guitar.

I knew.

How had I not figured it out before? How had I been so incredibly easy to trick?

My stomach clenched as I raced through the apartment, rushing into the bedroom, heading toward the nightstand beside the bed.

I heard him following, but I didn't turn to look. I couldn't look at him. Not yet.

I had to make sure what I knew was real and I wasn't losing my ever-loving mind. I dropped to my knees, ignoring a sting of pain, in front of the nightstand and yanked open the bottom drawer. I reached far into the back and pulled out a white envelope and dumped the contents out onto the floor.

I shuffled through the images, flinging them every which way until the one I was seeking caught my eye. I sat back on my haunches and stared down at it, like it was cursed and if I touched it, I might turn to stone.

Why hadn't I thought of this sooner?

Because it's insane. Because this is the stuff that only happens in movies.

I could feel him standing behind me, silent, waiting…

My fingers closed around the cool finish of the four-by-six paper and I pushed off the floor and turned.

I looked down at it again, waves of hair falling over my shoulders and concealing my face from sight. Two little boys, about the age of seven, sat arm in arm on a brick wall. Both were grinning happily and clutching red, white, and blue popsicles in their hands.

They looked exactly the same.

Both had dark, thick hair that curled around their faces. Their eyes were dark and fringed with impossibly dark lashes. Their skin was tanned from the sun, their lips bright red from the popsicle, and they were both dressed in blue-jean shorts with red-and-white striped T-shirts.

They were brothers.

They were twins.

I flipped the photo over and looked at the writing on the back.

Tucker and Max, brothers forever.

I lifted my eyes to stare at the man who had been living in my home. Who I woke up wrapped around. He looked utterly different to me now.

The eye sees what it expects to see. How many times had I cautioned a jury about this? How many times did I tell them to look past what they thought was obvious, to look past what they expected to see?

His face seemed sharper, more chiseled, and it wasn't because his hair was shorter. His eyes held some kind of hardness that a person only got from experience. His shoulders were broader, his chest slightly more muscular. And his abs… his abs were more defined.

Along with the tattoo that I knew decorated his back, he had a band around his left bicep. A black, solid stripe wrapped around the muscle and in the center were the words Semper Fi.

"Tucker," I said, holding the image between us. Max didn't talk about his twin very often, but he told me about him when we first starting dating. He said they looked exactly the same but couldn't be more different. I always thought I might meet Tucker someday…

But never like this.

He glanced at it but made no move to take it from my hand. When he looked, I saw stark pain flash across his features and his chest expanded with indrawn breath.

"Where is Max?" I said, this horrible feeling making me feel heavy. "What the hell did you do with Max?"

Tucker lifted his eyes from the photo and looked at me.

I knew whatever he was going to say was not going to be good.

The photo fluttered to the ground, drifting over beside the bed, when I launched myself at him. I hit his warm, solid chest head on, barreling into him with all my weight.

He didn't even move.

"Where is he!" I demanded, hitting his chest with the sides of my fists.

"Let's go sit down," he said, trying to lead me toward the living room.

"I'm not doing anything until you tell me about Max!" I yelled, yanking away from him and planting my feet into the floor.

Tucker spun around, pinning me with a hard and angry stare. "Max is dead."

Shock hit me like a bucket of ice-cold water.

Silence descended upon the room like it had been plunged into darkness. It was a thick and charged silence, the kind that made it hard to breathe.

"You're lying." I accused.

"I wish to God I was."

The pain behind his words wasn't something that could be pretended. The naked grief he didn't bother to conceal in his chocolate eyes couldn't be denied.

"No," I said, my voice a mere whimper.

"I'm sorry," he said, his voice gravelly and low.

Tears swam into my eyes, blocking my vision, and grief bubbled up inside me. Max was dead. My best friend in the world was gone and I hadn't even known it. I went about my life like everything was fine. I worked. I ate. I slept. I didn't question the gut feeling I had that something was different. I didn't realize something could be wrong.

Dear God, I kissed his brother.

I liked it.

The floodgates opened and tears rained down my cheeks. A sob ripped out of my throat and I placed my palm over my mouth to try and contain the sobs.

Grief like this couldn't be contained.

The pain and loss of losing someone you loved was too powerful to hold inside.

My shoulders slumped and shook as I cried and tears dripped onto my blouse. How easily your entire world can shift in just moments.

I felt his heat first, like a warm blanket that just came out of the dryer. His warmth radiated between us, and I swayed. Tucker wrapped his arms around me, pulling me into his bare chest, pressing a hand against the back of my head and holding me tightly.

I cried harder because I liked it.

I cried harder because his touch felt so good.

I was an awful person.

My boyfriend died and his brother came into this house, pretending to be him, and I didn't even know it.

What's more is I told him just earlier that I liked the "new" him better.

My back spasmed with every sob, sobs that now came out silent. It was as if my body didn't have the energy to make sound.

"Shhh," Tucker crooned, rocking us back and forth as we stood in the center of the bedroom with photos and papers scattered at our feet.

My tears leaked all over his skin, dampening his chest acting as a tissue for my grief. He didn't complain. In fact, it seemed like he held me tighter. It was the kind of hold that anchored a person, the kind of hold that made me feel like even though I was falling apart, all of my pieces were going to stay where they belonged.

I sobbed for a long time, until my eyes ran out of water and my throat hurt. Even after I began to quiet, he still held me. We still rocked back and forth in a comforting rhythm until little by little my brain began to work again.

Little by little reality came back, pushing into my fuzzy head and past my swollen eyes. My body felt drained and exhausted. But even my poor physical condition couldn't stop my brain from wanting to know everything.

I had to know.

I pulled away and looked up. "I want to know everything."

Tucker searched my eyes for long moments and then gave a short nod. "Come on."

I followed him out into the living room and tucked myself into the corner of the sofa. When I bent my knees to tuck my legs under me, they burned with pain. I looked down and realized for the first time since coming home that both my knees were raw and bloody.

It must have happened outside when we were being mugged.

The blood had dried, but my movements cause the cuts to split back open and were both oozing bright-red blood.

Instead of pulling my legs beneath me, I stretched them out and rested my feet on the coffee table.

I looked up to see the muscle in Ma—Tucker's jaw jump, and he went quietly into the bathroom. I heard the opening and closing of the cabinet and he reappeared with a small first aid kit.

I glared at him. "My knees are not important right now."

He laid the kit beside my feet and sat down beside me. He didn't lean back, but sat forward, resting his elbows on his knees. From this angle, I could see the broad expanse of his muscular back and a clear view of the tattoo that made me realize he wasn't Max.

In a single line down the right side of his back were five black stars. Each one looked exactly the same.

I watched them move as he reached forward and unlatched the kit, laying out some supplies on the wooden coffee table.

"Tucker," I said, halting his first aid attempt and grabbing onto his arm. "Tell me."

He abandoned the Band-Aids and ointment, sitting up and looking forward, keeping his gaze directed away from me.

"A couple days ago, the FBI showed up on my doorstep. They wanted me to step into Max's life, to tell no one, and to finish what he started."

"The FBI asked you to come here?"

He nodded.

"Max didn't just die, did he? He was murdered." The FBI didn't knock on just anyone's door.

"Yes, and I'm going to get the bastards who took his life from him." He vowed, sounding deadly calm and utterly serious.

"Does this have to do with his job?" I knew that lately Max had been under more pressure than usual, but he would never open up and tell me what was going on. I should have pushed harder. I shouldn't have taken no for an answer. If I hadn't, maybe Max would still be alive.

"Apparently some of the higher ups at his firm were involved in corporate espionage and money laundering. The Feds went to Max to work undercover—as a mole of sorts—to get physical evidence of the crimes."

"How could he agree and not talk to me about it! I could have helped him!" I all but shouted and shot up from the couch. I couldn't sit still another moment. I began pacing the living room, thinking of the ways I could have helped him.

I was a lawyer for God's sake. I worked for one of the most powerful and influential law firms in New York City. I could have helped him gather the information he needed. There were ways to gather information quietly so no one had to know.

"I don't think the Feds gave him much choice," Tucker said, grim.

"So he went undercover and the people he was trying to bring down found out and killed him for it" I surmised.

"Yes."

"How do you fit into all of this?" Maybe I was still muddy headed from the crying and everything else that happened tonight, but I wasn't making the connection.

"Before Max died, he got the evidence the Feds needed to put these guys away."

"Why aren't they in jail, then!" I demanded. The lawyer in me started thinking of the case I could build and what judge would be the best to reside over the case.

"Because the Feds don't know where he hid the flash drive with the evidence on it."

I stopped pacing and looked at him. "And they sent you here to find it."

He nodded.

Realization slammed into me. "That's why they came for me," I said to myself, the missing piece from my attempted kidnapping finally falling into place.

"What?" Tucker said.

"They think I know where it is," I whispered.

"What the hell are you talking about!" Tucker demanded, standing up from the couch.

I told him about the night the men came into the apartment and tried to drag me away. He listened with a gloomy look on his face.

As I talked, I thought of something else. "Those men tonight, they weren't really trying to mug us, were they?"

"No. When I walked into the office today, quite a few people were surprised I was still breathing. They intend to finish the job. They don't know where the drive is either, and they want us dead before we can take it to FBI."

"We have to find that drive. Those men who killed Max have to pay."

Tucker glanced at me, a determined look spreading across his features. "My thoughts exactly."

19

Tucker

Her tears unnerved me. I was use to grief, but I wasn't used to seeing it so clearly displayed.

I hadn't pegged her as an emotional type, so the feeling of her cool tears against my chest and the sound of her body-wracking sobs came as somewhat a surprise.

But in a sick way, her tears relieved some of my own sorrow. It was nice to be able to share that he was gone with someone. It felt good that there was now someone else who felt the absence of my brother like a bullet wound to the chest.

When she cried, I held her, not because I was hoping she would cry less, but because her tears were my tears. She didn't know it, but Charlotte cried for both of us. The release of her sadness somehow released some of my own. I hadn't realized how heavy of a burden carrying his death was. How truly angering it was watching the world go on around me as if nothing changed, when in fact everything was changed.

Finally, someone else understood. And while I didn't wish the pain of death on anyone, I was relieved I didn't have to feel it alone.

Except now she was in danger.

More danger than anyone realized. Those men came for her the night they killed my brother. They came for us again tonight. Now more than ever I was sorry I bated Wallace Jr. today because if Charlotte paid the price, I would never forgive myself.

"Have you looked through the apartment?" she asked, studying the room.

"Yes. And Max's office. But we can look here again. You might think of places to look that I hadn't."

She nodded and the movement caused her to sway just slightly on her feet.

"You need to sit down." I told her, standing up.

Her eyes went directly to my chest.

I ignored the flash of heat in my system and turned away, going to the kitchen to retrieve some water bottles from the fridge. "Here," I said, placing it in her hand and guiding her to the couch.

I studied her bloodied knees as she uncapped the water and took a drink. It seemed like forever ago those guys jumped us. It seemed like I'd been here for weeks, rather than days.

I heard a sniffle and I glanced at her. She was crying again.

Damn, women were leaky.

There wasn't anything I could say so I kept my mouth shut. I was likely doing her a favor anyway. I wasn't the kind of guy who had an arsenal of pretty words to make a girl melt. My arsenal was loaded with guns. And grenades.

But I was good at dressing a wound.

I sat forward, grabbing up an antiseptic wipe and ripping it open with my teeth. The smell reminded me of the battalion aid station (otherwise known as BAS) when I was enlisted and had to go to sick call.

"We don't have time for that," Charlotte said, glaring at the wipe.

"So you're one of *those* patients." I quipped.

"Excuse me?" She sniffed.

"The kind who battles the nurse even when they're just trying to help."

"Are you comparing yourself to a nurse?" she asked, lifting a delicately arched brow.

"I have an excellent bedside manner." I wagged my eyebrows at her.

She smiled, but then it quickly fell away. Guilt clouded her eyes.

"Smiling doesn't make you any less sorry that he's gone." I told her quietly, sitting on the table directly in front of her and reaching for her leg.

"I know, but it feels wrong."

"I get that," I said. It was the truth. Sometimes living after someone else dies was worse than the pain of them not being there.

I eased my hand around her knee, cupping the sensitive skin and drawing her leg out so her foot rested on the edge of the table in between my legs.

"This will probably sting."

I didn't wait for more of her protests, but began cleaning away the dried blood. It was still lightly bleeding and I got angry all over again for what those guys outside tried to do.

Jackasses.

It took two wipes to clean the area and then I dried it gently with a piece of gauze. Because it was still oozing blood, I chose a large Band-Aid and covered the pad with a thin layer of antibiotic cream. She said nothing as I smoothed the large patch over the scraped and bruised area carefully. If my fingers lingered over the silkiness of her skin, neither of us acknowledged it.

Then I reached for her other knee. When I lifted it into place I couldn't help but notice the goose bumps raised along her flesh. I glanced up; she was watching me.

"Are you cold?"

"A little," she said, glancing away.

I snagged a blanket off the side of the couch and motioned for her to sit forward so I could wrap the softness around her shoulders. When she leaned back, I tucked the ends around her, over her arms but taking care to leave her hands free so she could hold the water.

The blanket slipped off one arm when I pulled away and I hurried to push it back into place.

My hand brushed over her breast.

Little sparks of electricity shot up and down my limbs. Her indrawn breath caused my insides to tighten. Slowly, I withdrew my hand, the back of it brushing up against her again, and it was impossible not to notice the way her nipple responded even through her clothes.

I remembered the perfection of those dark pink nipples, the way they puckered right in the center of her full, perky mounds…

And I shouldn't be thinking this way.

I turned my attention back to her knee, ripping open another antiseptic wipe. As I ripped, it flew out of my hand and landed on the floor between the sofa and the table. I bent forward to retrieve it.

The sudden movement caused her foot to brush right up against my cock.

I jerked like someone threw scalding hot water on me. The desire was instantaneous. The need was overwhelming. Of course I began to grow hard; the single brush of her against that part of me was enough to make me come in my pants.

I swear since the second I laid eyes on her, every moment we shared had been some kind of foreplay. Never had any woman teased me so badly without even meaning to.

I snatched up the wipe and sat back, making sure her foot was not within touching distance of my pecker. 'Course the damage was already done.

I didn't look at her for fear it would just make me throb more. Instead, I focused solely on her scrapes and getting her injury cleaned up. She made a slight hissing sound when I swiped at the open wound, and I gentled my touch, realizing I was taking my sexual frustration out on her.

"Sorry," I murmured, still not looking up.

The abrasions on this knee weren't quite as bad as the other. It was not bleeding at all. After a little bit of internal debate, I decided not to cover this one, choosing instead to let the air get to it.

"Are you hurt anywhere else?" I asked, putting aside all the supplies and finally raising my eyes to hers. They seemed greener than before, as if the green specks inside the hazel had expanded.

"Nowhere that a Band-Aid can heal." Her cheeks were still wet from her tears.

Gently, I placed her foot back on the ground, and then I reached up to wipe away what was left of her sorrow.

She turned her cheek into my touch.

My heart literally stalled in my chest.

"I can't believe he's really gone," she whispered.

The pad of my thumb grazed the top of her cheekbone.

"Someone tried to kill me the night he died. They tried to kill me tonight."

"They won't stop until we're dead or they're in jail."

"So much death," she said. "I need some life."

Her eyes flicked up to meet mine. The need was unmistakable. Her desire mirrored my own. My touch turned not so gentle and the next thing I knew, I was yanking her forward to cover her mouth with mine.

First contact singed me and I groaned. Her lips were like a hot cup of coffee on a cold winter's day: warm and welcoming. Her passion slid all the way down my throat and coated my insides, lighting me up like a match and setting my blood on fire.

I pushed my tongue past her lips and swept inside her mouth, exploring the sharp edges of her teeth, the smoothness of her inner cheeks, and the texture of her tongue. I didn't stop kissing her even when my lungs begged for air. I needed her kiss far more than my lungs needed oxygen.

When at last I pulled back enough to draw a ragged breath, she made a sound of protest and came forward, catching my lower lip between her teeth and sucking it back into her moist mouth and rolling it around her tongue.

I shoved my hands beneath her arms and pulled her roughly into my lap. She straddled me with ease, wrapping those long legs around my waist and pushing herself more fully into my lap. When my hard length brushed against her middle, she shivered and rocked against me.

Our teeth smacked together when I deepened the kiss, slipping my tongue just a little farther inside her mouth. I wanted to be in her; I wanted as much of me as I could get inside her.

With both hands I squeezed her ass and she rocked against me again, making a little sound of pleasure. Charlotte broke the kiss and sat back, looking at me with eyes wide and swollen lips.

"It's never felt like this before," she said, her voice a low whisper.

"Darlin', you haven't felt anything yet."

I knew then I was going to sleep with her. I was going to have sex with Charlotte and I was going to enjoy every single second of it.

She was going to enjoy every single second of it.

There would be no more death tonight. There would be life.

And lots and lots of sex.

20

Charlotte

He reached for the end of the fabric tied into a bow at the side of my neck.

I didn't stop him.

Slowly, he pulled, dragging out my anticipation and creating an agonizing ache between my thighs. When the bow was no more, he abandoned the strips of silk, parting them and sliding his fingers around to deftly open the buttons at the base of my neck.

Everywhere he touched I felt the kiss of longing. The only thought in my head in that moment was, *Don't stop.*

When he reached for the hem of my shirt and glanced at me for permission, I could do nothing but nod my head.

He didn't have to be told twice. The silk was lifted up and away, disappearing where I couldn't see it. His hands curved around my hips as his eyes drank me in.

"Holy fuck, Charlie. You're gorgeous." He said it like a prayer, like he somehow stumbled across something sacred.

My knees began to tremble. The need within me was so great my body was having a hard time keeping it in.

Tucker released my sides and drew his hands upward, toward my gray-and-white satin pushup bra. I knew my chest was amply displayed for him, the tops of my creamy breasts peeking out from the soft fabric.

Both his palms slid over my breasts, covering them, squeezing them lightly. He released a ragged breath and began to knead them, massaging them with his fingers and thumbs. My skin began to tingle and this incredible urge to arch my back to display them even more shamefully filled me.

He dipped his fingers beneath the edges of the fabric and yanked the cups down. It was a lightning fast, abrupt movement. The bra was still hooked around my torso and the material bunched beneath my breasts, pushing them upward toward his touch. The cool air brushed over my already heated skin and I felt my nipples tighten.

The ends of my hair hung loose, tickling the already swollen and sensitive touch, giving me the urge to shake my head just to feel the silky strands heighten my pleasure even further. But Tucker wanted to be the one to deliver my pleasure.

He used the backs of his hands to push my hair back over my shoulders and flicked his thumbs across each of my hard nipples. I jolted with bliss and his mouth curved upward in an all-knowing smile.

It was as if he knew all the secrets to my body and he couldn't wait to share them all with me.

He continued the exquisite torture tracing a wide circle around my nipples, dragging his nails lightly across the skin and then pinching them both at exactly the same time.

I gasped as warm liquid slicked the inside of my panties. My skirt had ridden up, exposing some of the white cotton of my crotch, and I inhaled, noting the air around us was beginning to smell heady with the scent of desire.

He bent his dark head to take my breast into his mouth.

I stopped thinking.

He suckled at the delicate flesh, pulling it into his mouth and rubbing over it with his tongue. Then he would release it to lick at my nipple like it was some kind of delicious dessert. Just when I thought he would move to the next one, he reached around to deftly unhook the material and toss it away, completely baring my torso. My breast filled his hand completely when he palmed it, lifting it up so he could dive down to lick and suck the underside.

I moaned and my head fell back. Giving in, I arched my back, offering up every inch of my chest to his lips.

As his mouth worked my nipple, nipping at its hardness and then lapping at it with his slightly rough tongue, his hands slid around my bottom, where he took handfuls of my butt and squeezed. The motion caused me to rock against him, my slick heated crotch coming into contact with the rigid length of his penis.

Tucker stood abruptly, not letting me go, and started toward the bedroom. I anchored my legs around his waist and hung on for the ride. As he walked, his mouth found my other breast and he sucked it into his mouth and growled. The sound vibrated my flesh and I pushed myself farther against his mouth.

I felt swollen with need. Shaky and desperate for release.

The bedroom was dark, the only light in the room coming from out in the hall. Tucker laid me across the bed, kneeling between my thighs and looking down at my half-naked body.

I practically squirmed under his stare, not because I didn't like it, but because I did.

Tucker gathered my wrists together and raised them up above my head, anchoring them against the mattress with one of his hands. The weight of his body came over me, his bare chest brushing against mine when he claimed my mouth with his.

He kissed with a passion I had never known. The way his lips seemed to know every single angle, every single pressure point, made me want to beg for more. He kissed me long and deep; he kissed me short and brief. He kissed the corner of my mouth, dragging his lips across my jawline where he buried his face in my neck.

Teeth nipped at my earlobe and his voice whispered naughty phrases that no one had ever whispered to me before.

"I'm going to spread your legs wide and you're going to feel every inch of me."

I squirmed beneath him. I tried to free my hands. I yearned to scrape my nails down his back, feel the way his muscles bunched, and hold his face when he kissed me.

But he wouldn't let me move. He anchored me to the bed and all I could do was endure the sweet torture he bestowed upon my body. His tongue traveled down my neck where his teeth nipped and scraped. I shivered so much that my body settled into a continuous tremble. He drew his tongue downward, tracing a path between my breasts all the way down to my stomach, where his tongue circled my belly button and then slid off to the side.

I tried to squeeze my thighs together, but he wasn't going to have it. Instead, he pulled his knee up, pushing it right into my wet panties and using the pressure of his thigh to add heat to the fire. His mouth increased pressure as he pulled a mound of flesh from my belly into his mouth and sucked, creating minimal pain that had me gasping for more.

As he sucked that certain spot, he moved his knee around, grinding it against me as my stomach muscles clenched.

I was panting by the time he released me.

Using his hands, he spread my thighs as far as my skirt would allow and pressed gentle kisses to the inside of my legs. He licked along the edge of my panties, in that hollow part where my thigh meets my body, and I called out his name, delving my fingers deep into his dark hair.

He sat back, placing the heel of his hand on my swollen clit, and began rubbing in a circular motion, teasing it, using the wetness of my own panties to further increase my pleasure.

My back arched up off the mattress and his mouth captured my breast once more. I wanted to touch him. My mind kept whispering to reach out and grab a handful of his sexiness.

But I couldn't.

My desire—my need—was so intense that it made my body heavy. It made my brain sluggish. The only thing I could do was let wave after wave of pleasure roll through me.

Tucker sat back, towering over me like some kind of master to stare down at me through the darkness. Watching my face, he lowered the zipper on the side of my skirt, slipping his hands in the waistband, pulling it down over my hips and legs. I couldn't control the way my legs were shaking. I tried to still them, but it was no use. It was almost as if I was no longer in control of my own body, but he was.

He didn't say a word when he removed my panties, dragging them over my body until they were completely gone and I was totally exposed.

A sound echoed from the back of his throat and his fingers delved into the short, groomed curls just above the entrance to my body. Lightly he stroked the skin there, like he was studying some sort of map.

I reached for the belt on his trousers, wanting to see what was creating such a tent in the front of his pants. He snatched my hand away and brought it up, pressing a kiss to my fingertips and shaking his head no.

Tucker guided my hand away from him and brazenly placed it on the folds of my vagina. My skin immediately became slick with the juices from my body.

"I want to see you touch yourself."

He wanted me to touch myself.

I never touched myself. It was something I just never had done. Maybe he understood that, or maybe he just wanted to be involved, but he took my pointer finger and began sliding it up and down my folds. I cried out.

"You're soaking wet," he purred, and I felt a flash of satisfaction that my body pleased him.

He drew back his hands and grabbed my hips and lifted, gently flipping me over. My stomach fluttered with nervous energy because I had no idea what he was planning to do.

But I trusted him.

I trusted him completely.

His weight came over me again, pressing me into the blankets and brushing the hair off my neck. His tongue teased along the back of my hairline, licking and then blowing over the moistened area.

I wiggled a little under the attention, my body seeking something more. His hips settled against my bottom, stilling the action but creating even more yearning inside me. He raked his hands over my back, down the curve of my spine. Then he sat back to knead my buttocks, and I moaned his name.

The next thing I knew he was settling back over me, his chest against my back with his elbows resting on either side of me, surrounding me totally.

He was no longer wearing his pants. The unmistakable hardness of his bare erection and the rough texture of the hair nestled between his thighs brushed against my bare ass and caused me to moan.

He kissed my cheek, the corner of my eye. His tongue delved into my ear and he drew the lobe into his mouth.

"I want to feel you from the inside," he whispered in my ear.

I whimpered. God, I had never in my entire life wanted anything as much as I wanted him inside me.

One of his hands slid down my body and reached between the mattress and my pelvis. He lifted so my hips were tilted upward and his fingers probed into the nest of my curls. Holding me in that position, I felt the swollen crest of him tease my opening. My hands twisted in the blankets as his finger brushed over my swollen clit making it throb even more with sweet anticipation.

He pushed inside me with a single stroke. I moaned and buried my face in the blankets, trying to stifle the amount of noise I was making. I couldn't help it.

So. Damn. Good.

His penis was rock hard and it strained against the walls of my vagina, stretching me out and filling me up.

In my ear, his breath was ragged as he slowly began to move. In and out, in and out. He kept his body against mine so we experienced full body contact along with his amazing thrusts. He kissed across my shoulder blades; he kissed the back of my neck.

My juices coated his cock with ease and he slid back and forth, creating friction and causing a build-up of epic proportions.

It was entirely erotic that I could feel him, that I knew how large and how hard he was… but I had yet to lay eyes on the member that delivered such sweetness.

Then he pulled away and I was left with this aching sadness that almost made me weep. "Turn for me, darlin'," he said.

I did so eagerly, flipping over and fastening my gaze on his magnificent naked body. He was thick and lengthy, the hardened flesh jutted out from his body like a warrior primed for battle.

Before I could look my fill, he settled between my thighs and pushed inside me once more. Little chills of ecstasy raced across my skin. I wrapped my arms around his back, digging my nails into the smooth skin stretched over muscle as he pounded inside me.

The muscles inside me began to contract and he balanced himself on his hands, looking down at me as he continued to move.

"I want you to cum now," he commanded.

It was like he flipped a switch inside my body. An orgasm exploded through me, causing me to cry out over and over again as wave after wave of bliss rocked me.

I felt him stiffen, his body going rigid as he shoved his arm beneath me, lifting my languid body off the mattress and gathering me close. I felt his release pump inside of me. My body welcomed it; my body craved it. His stifled moan was like a symphony to my ears.

And then he collapsed on top of me. I could feel the erratic beating of his heart as satisfaction filled my every cell.

I'd never known.

I'd never imagined.

This was the stuff movies were written about.
This was the stuff that I thought only lived in books.

It wasn't just a fairytale.

It was real.

21

Tucker

Best. Sex. Ever.

And I've had a lot of sex in my life, so for me to be lying here (still on top of the woman even) and be instantly craving more is saying something.

Damn, she made the perfect partner. She let me take the lead, she let me ravish her body, and the sounds she made… the sounds about drove me wild. Her body was tight and my cock fit inside her like a sports car in a custom garage. Like she was made just for me.

Just replaying what happened between us had me stirring to life with renewed energy. My arms were still wound around her body. I was likely crushing her, but she didn't complain. I slid out of her moist heat, my dick hating me for it, and I started to pull away.

Her eyes fluttered open and she looked up, giving me a relaxed smile. It was the most relaxed I'd ever seen her. God, she was beautiful. I dipped my head, connecting our mouths to press a full, gentle kiss to those heart-shaped lips.

I rolled off her, taking up residence on the empty side of the bed.

I just kissed her… willingly. The thought had my stiffening cock softening and my mind wondering what the hell was wrong with me.

I never kissed women after we did the deed.

I never laid on her either. Usually I got up and went home, or if I was still drunk, I rolled over and went to sleep.

I never said I was the romantic type.

Which I guess is why my behavior seemed odd. Kissing and touching usually made me uncomfortable. I had sex for the release, for the pure pleasure that it gave my body. I didn't do it because it gave me butterflies in my belly or made my heart go pitter patter.

That shit was for girls.

So why was I lying here thinking about threading her fingers through mine? Why was I already anticipating the next time I could bury myself inside her?

I felt her shift beside me and I turned my head. Charlotte lay on her side, facing me with her fine-boned hand curled up on the pillow beside her. There was just enough light for me to make out her features, the way her hair spread out across the pillow.

For the first time in a very long time I wished I was better at this. I wished I knew something I could say, some pretty words that she would like to hear.

The hand resting between us lifted and her cool fingers stroked the side of my face lightly. Before pulling away, she cupped the side of my jaw and her lips curved upward.

I didn't have to say anything. No pretty words would compete with what we just did… and how that singular touch made me feel. So I settled for just watching her, for the glimpses I could catch in the dark.

Once again my cock starting stirring. Clearly, it wasn't done with her. Clearly, one epic sex session was not going to be enough.

Why her? something inside me asked. Why would the one woman that was supposed to be off limits be the one I wanted more of?

The reason didn't matter because it didn't change anything.

Charlotte was my brother's girlfriend. I broke the brother code by sleeping with her tonight. Yeah, maybe I could pass tonight off as too much beer, too much emotion, and being attacked on the street. Or I could chalk it up to being temporarily insane because my twin was gone.

All of those reasons were much better than admitting to myself that I was the world's biggest ass.

I wondered what Charlie was thinking right about now.

She was looking at me, her breathing even and her face relaxed. She was probably thinking about how great in the sack I was.

The longer we lay there, the farther away we got from the "afterglow" of sex. The air around us began to change, to become more tense, and the satisfied impression I picked up on from her side of the bed began to diminish.

I knew exactly what was going on.

She was starting to have regrets. Reality was crashing in from our spur-of-the-moment sex, and she was looking at me and seeing me… not Max.

The realization stung, and the thought that maybe I wasn't good enough for her created a bitter taste in my mouth.

"I'm going to take a shower," she said after a while. She slid over to the vacant side of the bed and stood, dragging the sheet with her, and tucked it around her naked form.

I would be lying if I said I wasn't disappointed I wasn't going to get to watch her luscious ass retreating.

Charlotte walked across the bedroom where she stopped in the door. Ahead of her, the light from the other rooms shone, creating a golden halo effect around her, making her look like just a shadow. She rested a hand on the doorframe and looked over her shoulder, her hair cascading down her back.

I couldn't see her eyes in this kind of light, but I felt them.

And then she turned and walked into the bathroom, quietly shutting the door behind her. The closing of that door signaled our time was over. This was usually my cue to leave. To throw on my clothes, climb in my truck, and drive home.

I threw off the remaining blanket and stood. My pants were lying on the floor at the end of the bed.

I ignored them.

I wasn't getting dressed.

The shower was already running when I let myself into the bathroom. The white sheet was lying in crumpled heap on the floor and steam was wafting up from behind the curtain, dissipating in the air, creating humidity in the small room.

I felt angry for some reason. Cheated. I didn't like it and I wasn't going to accept it.

The shower curtain made a sharp scraping sound when I yanked it across the rod. Charlotte gasped and leapt back beneath the spray. For several long seconds, I was transfixed with the water running freely over her naked skin.

"Tucker! What the hell are you doing?" she said, crossing her arms over her chest like she was embarrassed.

It was amusing. "I already know every inch of that chest intimately. Covering them up is a waste of energy," I said darkly.

"We shouldn't have done that," she said, turning her back on me completely. I got a nice view of her ass.

Anger burned my throat and I swallowed it down.

"Water is getting all over the floor," she fussed without turning around.

I stepped into the shower and pulled the curtain closed. The water was hot, scalding even. Like she was trying to wash me off her skin. I wouldn't allow it.

Charlotte spun, shock written across her features.

"You liked it," I said, a challenge in my tone.

Water poured over her head and dragged her hair down, and small drops of the liquid clung to her golden lashes.

"Tell me you liked it." I demanded.

"If I tell you, will you get out?"

I regarded her with stony silence. I wasn't promising one damn thing.

Eventually she sighed wearily. "Yes, I liked it." Her voice was low like she was whispering a secret.

"I'm not done with you yet."

Her eyes snapped up to mine and she pushed at the wet strands that had fallen in her eyes. "Yes, you are. We shouldn't have done that! You're Max's brother." At the mention of my brother, her lower lip wobbled and her shoulders slumped.

I hated to see the sorrow that swam within her. I wanted to kiss it away.

Yeah, it was wrong, but that's how I felt.

We stood there with water raining down around us, the drops splashing off her skin and landing on mine. It seemed we were at a stalemate.

"One night," I heard myself say.

"What?" she asked, leaning toward me ever so slightly.

"Give me one night with you. One night for us to get this attraction out of our system. One night without guilt, without telling ourselves how horrible we are." It made perfect sense. Charlotte was off limits to me, which is exactly why I wanted her so badly.

All we had to do was remove the barriers between us, the temptations. Our thirsts would be quenched and in the morning, neither of us would want the other.

I could see her thinking about it. I could see her weighing the pros and cons. I knew that in her mind, she was creating a neat little list and mentally checking off the boxes.

"And in the morning?" she asked.

"In the morning, I'll be Max's brother and you can help me find that drive. Once we hand it over, I'll go to North Carolina and you won't have to see me again."

"I loved him," she said, like she had to make sure I knew.

"I loved him, too."

I knew the exact moment when she gave in, when she decided to let me have the rest of the night. Something in my chest lightened. I felt as if a one hundred-pound weight had been removed from my shoulders.

"One night." She agreed.

I wasn't about to waste a single second. Surging forward, I wrapped my arms around her and spun, letting the spray cascade over my back and shoulders. The hot water slid between us, making our skin slide together. I took her mouth in a hungry kiss. I felt like a starved man, a man who had been without food for far too long.

Our tongues mingled together; our breath mixed. I tugged her lower lip into my mouth and sucked while her arms came up to grip my biceps. My hand found the heavy, wet mass of her hair and I grabbed a handful of it, tugging her head back to expose her throat.

I licked at the water running down the sensitive flesh of her neck, enjoying the way her body trembled. Reaching between us, I pinched her nipple and she arched toward me.

I brought our lips together once more, kissing her as deeply as I could.

Charlotte grew bold, her hand dipping low as she took my full hardness in her palm. Using the water from the shower, she began to stroke me, sliding up and down along the shaft and making the breath hiss between my teeth. My body jerked when she hit that sweet spot on my head, the most sensitive spot on my entire body.

My toes curled into the shower floor as her hand traveled lower to cup my balls in her warm and welcoming palm.

I loved the way her hands felt on me. I loved the way her touch was bold yet still tentative. I loved the careful way she stroked me as if being gentle was a form of worship.

After several long minutes of nothing but her touch, I couldn't take anymore. My blood began to boil; my cock began to demand more. I grabbed her face and tilted her head back to stare down into her eyes.

"This isn't going to be like the last time. I'm not going to take my time with you. I want you too badly. I want you here. Now."

"Then take me."

The words were barely out of her mouth when I moved. Within seconds, I had her legs wrapped around my waist and her back pinned against the wall of the shower. Water flowed over our bodies as I surged inside her already wet and ready vagina.

I cried out, burying my face in her neck, and stilled, allowing her body to stretch around me and allowing me a moment to catch my breath. Pure ecstasy rolled along my limbs. The feeling of her tight, warm walls clenching around me was almost enough to get me to spill my seed.

Almost.

I wanted more.

"Hold on, darlin'," I drawled and began to pound inside her. She couldn't move because I had her trapped between me and the shower wall. I surged in her again and again, my thigh muscles burning from the effort and my penis so hard that it throbbed.

Charlotte thrashed her head from side to side, gasping for breath and asking for more.

I went deep into her, but I wanted deeper. I released some of the pressure on her body and she slid down the wall, burying the head of my cock into the most private places within her.

I couldn't hold it any longer and I titled, surging myself along her inner wall, and both of us fell over the edge.

Her nails bit into my back and her teeth sank into my shoulder. The little mewling sounds that released from her throat as she rocked against me were like music to my ears.

I started to pump again, milking every last drop of my orgasm that I could. When it was over, we collapsed against the wall, both of us breathing heavy. The water had turned cool, and I angled my back to keep most of the cold droplets from spraying her body.

When I finally stepped back to turn off the water, she slid down, like her legs were incapable of holding her up. I chuckled and pinned her once more to the wall while I shut off the cold spray and reached for her towel. I wrapped it around her body and then picked her up, stepping over the edge of the tub and carrying her out of the bathroom and back to bed.

"I'm soaking wet," she protested when I tried to lay her in the bed.

So I sat her on her feet and took possession of the towel. I dried every single part of her body. Twice.

After she returned the favor, we abandoned the towel and slid beneath the blanket. I gathered her close, marveling at how well her body fit up against mine. My hand cupped her ass, kneading the bare, round flesh.

"You better get some rest while you can." I warned her. "We still have the rest of the night and I'm not even close to being done with you yet."

"You promise?" she asked.

I smiled in the dark. It was a promise I would be thrilled to keep.

22

Charlotte

I didn't know there were so many different ways to have sex. Last night was an education of a lifetime. I had no idea where he learned some of the things he did to me, and frankly, I was afraid to ask.

But damned if they didn't feel good.

We did it on the bed, in the shower, against the wall, on the floor, and with him sitting in a chair and me straddling his lap.

He touched every inch of my body like he would be taking a written exam the next day and needed to know every last place that made me purr.

I'd never felt so sexually charged… so wanted.

Tucker made me feel bold. He made me feel like I could do anything to him and not be embarrassed. He was so daringly comfortable with his body that I somehow forgot to be uncomfortable with mine. When I reached for his cock, his eyes would get heavy, his lids would droop, and he would whisper my name.

I loved when he whispered my name.

He asked me for one night and I was so incredibly glad I gave it to him. For hours upon hours I didn't think of deadlines or work. I didn't worry about my suit getting wrinkled or my fine hair getting knotty. I didn't check my email every ten minutes, and I felt like I could breathe.

And now the darkness in the sky was giving way to the new light of day, slowly spreading across the horizon and turning the sky a deep shade of apricot.

My bare feet barely made a sound as I made my way into the dim kitchen. I don't think I slept for more than an hour last night, but I wasn't tired at all. I pressed the start button on the coffee maker and then turned to retrieve a carton of orange juice from the fridge.

The strong aroma of brewing coffee wafted through the air and I inhaled the rich scent as I filled a glass with juice.

Strong arms slid around me from behind, looping around my waist and drawing me back against a firm chest. I closed my eyes and tried to commit the way he felt to my memory. I didn't want to forget this.

Tucker nuzzled the side of my neck and then released me. I held the glass of OJ over my shoulder, offering him the drink.

He took it, and I busied myself with capping the carton and putting it away. I felt his eyes on me the entire time I moved. I felt the intensity of his dark gaze, the heat searing into my bones. Even though my lady parts were swollen and slightly sore, I would have welcomed him again without hesitation.

But it was morning.

Our one night together was ending.

After I poured some coffee in a mug and replaced the pot, I turned around to look at him.

He looked almost exactly like Max, but he was so incredibly different. I wanted to know more about him, more about his past, his feelings, his life.

You aren't dating him. I reminded myself. *You're dating his brother.*

At least I was… until he was murdered.

Emotion bubbled up inside me, threatening to overwhelm me, so I abandoned my mug and excused myself to the bathroom. I gripped the cold marble counter until my fingers turned white, bowing my head, and squeezed my eyes closed against all the thoughts and feelings jumbled up inside.

Being a lawyer, I knew I couldn't hide the truth from myself. The truth *always* came out.

I kept the death grip on the counter but forced my eyes up so I could look into the mirror. I barely recognized myself.

My skin was flushed and pink with mild brush burns from Tucker's unshaven face. My lips were swollen and full, my eyes clear and brighter than I'd ever seen them. My golden-blond hair was a tangled mess, waving down over my shoulders and across my chest.

I was used to seeing someone much more pulled together, someone with tightly pulled-back hair, focused eyes, and pale, unmarked skin.

I looked so much younger this way, so much more relaxed… happy.

It made me feel incredibly guilty.

How could I look so happy? How could I feel so relaxed when I just found out that Max was dead?

More still, how could I have slept with his brother—his twin?

I was a skanky, dirty, no-good ho.

Technically, I hadn't cheated on Max, and in the world of the law, a technicality was more than enough to get someone acquitted. But this wasn't a court of law and what I did was still a betrayal.

A single tear tracked its way over my cheek and rolled until it dripped off my face and fell onto the counter.

For days I had been living here with Tucker, so blinded by my attraction for him, so in awe of the sudden onslaught of desire that tangled me up inside I never stopped to really examine the evidence. If I had I would have known it wasn't Max. I would have known that something was wrong.

"I'm so sorry, Max. For so many things," I whispered, wiping more tears from my cheeks.

I couldn't change how I spent last night. In fact, I really didn't want to. Yes, I was ashamed that I would so quickly jump into bed with Tucker, but I didn't regret it. I couldn't. My body still hummed with satisfaction. I felt freed in a way I never had before.

That didn't mean I had to repeat it.

Tucker and my relationship (if you could call it that) from here on out was strictly about finding the evidence Max left behind and getting justice for his murder. After that, we would do exactly what Tucker said. We'd go our separate ways.

There was a soft knock on the bathroom door. "Did you fall in?" Tucker asked from the other side.

I rolled my eyes. He had the manners of a moose.

"No," I answered.

"Well, standing in there gripping the counter and feeling guilty isn't going to make anything better."

I paused. How could he be so barbaric one moment and the next be so oddly perceptive?

"Coffee's getting cold." He cajoled.

With a sigh, I opened the bathroom door and was greeted with a solid wall of man. Holy smokes, he had a nice chest, all wide and muscular. The tattoo on his arm constantly drew my eye.

He needed a shirt.

Like right now.

My coffee was clutched in his long, thick fingers. Something deep inside me tingled with the memory of how well he used those fingers…

I jerked myself out of my porn dream (What the hell was happening to me? Next thing I knew I would be Googling pictures of naked men on the internet. Gross.) and grabbed my cup, taking a long swig.

"We should talk," he said, his eyes turning serious.

We definitely needed to talk. "Yes, we should." I stepped around him and walked toward the living room, glancing behind me to make sure he was following. He wasn't. He was staring at my legs.

I needed some pants.

And a shirt that wasn't his. A shirt that didn't smell just like him.

I changed course and went directly into the bedroom, setting my coffee down and stepping over all the papers and photos I dumped on the floor last night to get a pair of leggings and a sweater. I guess I would just skip the gym this morning. I would be glad for that if I didn't know myself well enough to realize that me skipping today would equal a longer workout tomorrow.

I hesitated before pulling off the T-shirt I was wearing, but then I felt silly. It wasn't like he hadn't already seen the merchandise.

"So we need to find a flash drive that contains evidence of corporate espionage that Max hid somewhere so the Feds can put away the men who killed him?" I summed up and spun around, tugging the ends of my hair out of the neck of my shirt.

"Yeah," Tucker said, reaching for my coffee and taking a drink.

The sight of his lips wrapping around the rim of the mug gave me little shivers. I had a stark memory of him pulling my finger into his mouth and then slowly drawing his lips down to the tip.

"Charlie," he called, his voice breaking into the erotic thought.

I glanced up, my cheeks heating with embarrassment because I got caught in the act of reliving what we did last night. "Yeah?" I asked, hoping he didn't realize what I was thinking about.

A devious little smile curved his very talented mouth. He knew. Of course he knew. "I said, do you have any idea where Max might have put a flash drive in this apartment?"

I knew where Max kept everything. I knew how he liked to fold his socks. I knew his favorite kind of shampoo. That he didn't like to use the oddball fork in the silverware drawer because it had a "funny-shaped" handle. I knew the way he filed his papers, the shorthand language he used on his calendar, and his favorite tie.

And now he was never coming back.

Overwhelming sorrow expanded inside me, like a balloon being filled with too much air. The thought of never seeing him again, of never being able to talk strategy or watch movies together, left a gnawing kind of pain in the center of my chest.

I wondered if the sorrow would ever go away. I wondered if he could forgive me for how I spent my first night without him.

Even though he was gone, there was still something I could do for him. There was still a way I could at least attempt to make up for what I did.

I could bring down his killers. I could see their murdering asses in jail. Maybe I would arrange for them to have a cellmate named Tiny Tim, only he wouldn't be that tiny.

"If it's here, I'll find it." I vowed.

Tucker held the mug out to me as I passed by him. I glanced between him and my mug. The mug he practically just made out with.

Okay, so he didn't make out with it.

But his lips touched it. Same difference.

"Keep it," I said. "I'll get another."

His knowing chuckle followed me all the way out into the living room. I ignored him. I had a flash drive to find.

23

Tucker

We searched the entire place. Charlie looked in places I never even thought of. She knew all the little nooks and crannies in this place, and every single one of them was empty.

Not finding it was a letdown.

Going through all my brother's belongings was worse.

I missed him, and the fact we drifted apart during recent years was something I would never forgive myself for. The distance between us was my fault, a fact I never wanted to admit to myself until now.

It was obvious that Charlie cared for him. I could see the lines of pain etched in her pretty features. I watched the set of her shoulders slump every time she came across something that meant a lot to Max.

I was an ass. A world-class jerk.

I took advantage of her sorrow last night. I took advantage of her fear from being attacked. She was a willing participant, but I was the one who initiated it all.

"It isn't here," Charlotte said, bringing me out of deep thought.

"I already searched his office and his locker at the gym. He didn't have a safety deposit box at the bank. Can you think of anywhere else it could be? Was there anyone Max trusted—really trusted—that he might give it to for safekeeping?"

After a moment's thought, a light came into her eyes. "There is one place we can try."

"Great, let's go."

"We can't."

I swung back around, wondering if she lost her damn mind. "What the hell do you mean we can't?"

"The place doesn't open until later." She glanced at the clock and sighed. "Besides, I'm going to be late for work."

"You're going to work?" I asked incredulously.

"I have to. The clients that I managed to get an account with are coming in to sign the papers today. I have to be there."

"You're going to put your job ahead of justice for Max?" I growled.

She drew herself up to her full height (which was still shorter than me) and gave me a glare. "How dare you say such a thing to me?"

I crossed my arms over my chest.

"If I call in sick, it will look suspicious. I've never called in sick a day in my life. People will wonder what's going on. Whoever killed Max is probably watching us. The best thing to do is go on like everything is normal."

"I'm not going into his office and pretending to be him. That place sucks."

Charlie rolled her eyes and went back to the bedroom. I followed her. "Fine. Stay here and pick up the mess we made searching."

I raised an eyebrow. Did she just suggest I stay home and clean? Maybe I should bake some cupcakes with pink frosting while I was at it.

With an armload of clothes, she turned to me. "I'll go in, sit through the meeting, and then tell the partners I'm coming down with something and come home. By then, the restaurant will be open and we'll go see if Max took the drive there."

"It's at a restaurant?"

She nodded. "Max's best friend owns a restaurant here in the city. It's a really classy place."

Classy = no beer.

"I can't wait," I said sarcastically.

She grinned and went to the bathroom, shutting herself in. It was too bad because I was hoping for a glance of some skin.

A few minutes later, she came out dressed in a pair of loose black pants and what looked like a dark-green fitted T-shirt tucked into the pants. It accentuated her flat stomach and the way her waist curved in like an hourglass. Her hair was pulled back in that stupid bun.

She rushed to the door, sticking a pair of black high heels on her feet and grabbing a black fitted jacket. Her brief case was sitting by the door where she left it along with her purse.

"Charlie," I said, stopping her from leaving.

She turned back.

"About last night…" I began, not sure why I wanted to bring it up but unable to let her walk out of here without bringing it up. We hadn't talked about it at all. True to our agreement, when the sun came up, our focus switched to Max.

Focusing on Max was good. But looking at her now…

She held up her hand, halting my words and my thoughts. "It can't happen again."

Her words wounded my manly pride. That had been some stellar sex. I excelled in pleasing her. I knew we had an agreement, but I thought once she got a taste of this she'd want more.

So I did what any man with wounded pride would do. I lied.

"I wasn't talking about the sex," I said, clearing my throat. "I just wanted to remind you to be careful out there. Clearly those guys last night were following us. Waiting. Pay attention to your surroundings today. If anything seems out of the ordinary—anything at all—you get to a crowded area and you call me. Okay?"

A pink stain bloomed across her high cheekbones and she shifted uncomfortably. "Oh. Right."

I didn't enjoy making her feel like she was the only one that was thinking about the incredible sparks between us. But I didn't know what else to do. It was easier this way. Less painful.

She left the apartment without a single glance behind her.

I sighed and ran a hand over the top of my head.

I wondered what she would have said if I'd told her the truth. I wondered if the guilt in her eyes would give way to something more.

I wondered if I was the only one that thought one night hadn't been enough.

24

Charlotte

Muse was located in Manhattan in an old building that was completely rehabbed on the inside. It had soaring ceilings, exposed brick walls, glossy hardwood floors, and beams running overhead. The artwork on the walls was abstract and oversized; the tables were all chic and dark wood with real leather padding. Soft jazz music flowed through the surround system in the walls, and there was a giant, round freestanding bar in the center of the establishment that was comprised of mostly glass.

Cavalli Overcraft had been a serious business major for several years, with aspirations of working with the stock market. He even graduated with honors. Max and Cavalli were on the fast track to becoming corporate stars when Cavalli decided that the pressure and stress of the corporate world wasn't what he wanted out of life.

So he quit his job and went to culinary school to study his secret passion: food. Once he was finished, he put his business knowhow and connections he made while working in New York to good use and opened up Muse, where he was not only the owner, but the head chef.

The upscale setting yet relaxing atmosphere had people flocking to this place, and the food kept them coming back.

Most people thought Cavalli was completely insane. Secretly, I admired him.

Even though Max continued on with his career in the corporate world, he and Cavalli remained friends, and I would go as far as to say that Cavalli was probably the only real friend Max had.

Besides me, of course.

So when Tucker asked me if there was anyone Max would trust with the flash drive, I immediately thought of Cavalli.

"Nice place," Tucker said as we walked inside the building.

"Remember, you've been here before." I reminded him. Now that I knew he wasn't really Max, it was so completely obvious I couldn't help but worry someone else might realize.

"Should I have called ahead for a reservation?" he asked, leaning over to whisper in my ear. His breath brushed over the outside of my ear and I wanted to groan.

You'd think an entire night of nothing but sex would satisfy me for a good long time. It only seemed to make me crave it more.

"It's still early enough we shouldn't need one," I said, pushing aside my cravings to focus on the matter at hand.

We didn't have to wait long when a hostess dressed completely in black escorted us to a table on the far side of the room, behind the bar. She handed us each a menu and then went off, leaving us alone.

"Cavalli always comes out of the kitchen to talk with the guests. He'll see us and come over, and we can find out if he has it then," I told Tucker.

"I'm starving," he complained, looking over the menu.

I was hungry too. I hadn't eaten a thing all day. "We're here. We might as well eat."

After we ordered (a fresh green salad with shrimp for me and a steak for him), we sat there in silence, not really knowing what to say. It seemed like we'd already experienced a lot together, yet I hardly knew him at all.

"Max never talked about you," I blurted, because clearly I couldn't think of a more polite way to be rude.

"That doesn't surprise me," Tucker said, acting like my abrupt statement was normal. "We haven't been close for quite a few years."

"But why?" I questioned. "I thought twins were inseparable."

He half smiled. "We were as kids. But kids grow up. And Max and I were nothing alike."

"You're in the Marine Corps?" I asked, thinking about the tattoo on his arm.

"I was. I just got out last month. I was in about six years."

"Why did you get out?"

"I felt like it was time to move on. I was tired of being told where to live, what to wear, what to do."

"Sounds stifling."

"No more stifling than the life you're living."

His words cut into my chest and caught me by surprise. "My life isn't stifling."

The corner of his mouth lifted. "If you say so," he said, picking up his glass of iced tea. After he swallowed, he made a face at the glass. "I can't wait to get down South."

"You're going down South?"

He nodded. "Should be there now."

"Where?"

"Jacksonville, North Carolina. My buddy Nathan just moved there with his wife Honor. He used to be in the Corps too. We're opening up a private investigative firm. We already have some work the Corps hired us for."

"I've never been to the South before."

"It's warmer, the people are friendlier, and they know how to make a glass of sweet tea."

I could tell he was anxious to get there, to be in a place he really wanted to be. For some reason, that left me with a hard feeling in my stomach.

"So what happened between you and Max?" I asked.

He shrugged. "It's mainly my fault. He went off to college, became a big shot here, and I joined the Marines. He was always the golden boy out of the pair of us. The one who was going to be the most successful."

"I'd say serving your country is pretty impressive." I refuted. He almost sounded like he thought Max was better than him. Max never acted like he was better than anyone; he always treated everyone equally.

"It wasn't always easy." He got this faraway look in his eye.

"Did you ever go overseas?"

"Twice. Both of them war zones. I saw more than I cared to. A lot of good men died. Some of them my friends."

The waitress arrived then, causing us to halt the conversation. I couldn't help but sit there and think about the horrible things he'd likely seen. I didn't expect him to keep talking when the server walked away, but he did.

"Our convoy was attacked one day while en route to a new base. They blew the hummer in front of us right off the ground. Ripped it all apart. The guys inside died instantly."

I gasped and automatically reached across the table and laid my hand across his. He looked down at our joined hands silently for a moment and then glanced up.

Thinking I did the wrong thing, I began to slip my hand away. He flipped his over and captured my retreating fingers, slipping his through mine and giving them a squeeze.

"The driver of the hummer we were in stopped and the three of us got out, looking for the threat, for the men who killed our brothers."

"You got out!" I demanded. "Why didn't you speed away?"

He gave me a level look. "We don't leave men behind."

I nodded.

"The hummer that was hit lay about fifty feet away, and I ran to it while the others covered me. It was on fire and charred, but I had to be sure no one was left alive. The smell of their burning bodies… it's something I'll never forget."

I shivered, trying to picture a bunch of men in the center of a war zone, strapped with weapons and uniforms, traveling across the sand while bombs and gunfire aimed to take their lives.

"While I was checking the hummer, the one we had been riding in took a hit. The hit hadn't been head on like the previous one, and the passenger side of the vehicle blew out, causing it to roll. It rolled right over Govern, the man who'd been driving."

I set my fork down, unable to eat. "Then what happened?"

"Connors was standing out in the open, completely vulnerable to attack. So I left the cover of the burning hummer and raced toward him, meaning to cover him while he ran to safety. There were snipers up in a cluster of rocks not too far from where we were and they were picking us off with ease. Anyway, my movement distracted the shooter and the next shot went wild, bouncing off the sand in front of us. When I reached Connors, the sun glinted off the scope of the sniper's gun and I lined up a shot. I'll never forget that moment… My eyes connected with the man trying to kill us, and we stood there frozen for long moments, staring each other down through the scopes on our weapons."

"Tucker," I whispered, tears filling my eyes.

"We pulled the trigger at the same time." He blinked and looked up at me. "My bullet killed him. His bullet would have killed me, but Connors knocked me out of the way, taking it instead."

I gasped, thinking how incredibly close he had been to death. "And Connors?" I asked, praying to God he was okay.

"It was a gut shot," he said, grim. "He wasn't able to walk, so I carried him. I walked for ten miles before someone found us."

He carried a bleeding, injured man for ten miles through the desert, and every step he likely wondered if it would be his last. What kind of mental consequence did a situation like that have on a person?

"Did he die?" I whispered.

"It was a close call, but no, he didn't. He's still alive. He got out of the Corps after that and he lives out in North Dakota with his wife and son."

"You saved his life."

"He saved mine first."

Tucker glanced down at our joined hands and then glanced back up. "That experience changed me. Watching men I cared about, men who I considered family, die… It left an imprint on my soul, something that will always be there. I kind of broke away from people after that. I didn't get as close. I let relationships, like the one I had with Max, slip away. It was too hard to be close to people, too hard to love them."

"What about Nathan?" I asked, thinking of the friend he mentioned before.

He smiled, a genuine smile that lit up his eyes. "I've only known Nathan a couple of years. He kind of just became a fixture in my life. He understands war. He has scars of his own. For quite a while, it was just me and him."

"Didn't you say he's married?"

"To a writer. He saved her from being kidnapped. She wrote a book about it. They've been together ever since."

I felt my eyes go wide. "Are you talking about the book they made into a movie? *Text?*"

He grinned. "You've heard of it?"

"Everybody has heard of it."

He chuckled.

"I can't believe you're friends with Honor Calhoun," I said in awe. I loved her books. Well, when I got the time to read.

"It's Honor Reed now," he corrected.

The waitress came by and seemed concerned neither of us had touched our food. I assured her it was wonderful; we'd just been talking. She didn't seem convinced when she walked away.

"I shouldn't have let my relationship with Max suffer. I spent all that time avoiding being close to him, afraid that I might be killed on my next deployment, that it would only hurt him worse…"

"And then he died," I whispered.

"Yeah, and now I have a gut full of regret as well as a hole in my heart."

"If it makes a difference. Max never seemed angry at you. He never seemed like he felt betrayed."

"Thought he never talked about me."

"He didn't. Not really. But I would have known if your distant relationship hurt him."

"Thanks," he said lightly, expelling a breath.

I don't know if my words brought him any comfort, but I sincerely hoped they did. He'd been through a lot and it seemed that he didn't need anything else to think about in the dark of the night.

A man wearing a pristine white coat approached the table, and Tucker stiffened. I looked up and smiled. "Cavalli!" I said so Tucker would know who it was we were talking with.

Cavalli's face broke out into a wide smile. "Max! Charlotte!" he said, stopping beside the table. Tucker offered his hand and the two men shook before Cavalli leaned over and kissed my cheek.

"I have to say I am surprised to see you here. It's so early in the day. I thought you two workaholics didn't leave the office until at least seven."

"Well, both our calendars were clear this afternoon so we decided to be spontaneous," I replied.

Cavalli smiled. "Well, when the server told me we had guests not eating, I was alarmed! I thought there was something wrong with the food!"

"The food is perfect. We were just talking."

Cavalli glanced over at Tucker and I held my breath, wondering if he was going to realize it wasn't really Max. "Long time no see, Max! How's the corporate world treating you?"

Tucker smiled. "Busy as ever, Cavalli. The restaurant looks great. Looks more successful than the last time I was here."

I watched Cavalli for signs he thought something was off. He didn't appear to notice anything. I breathed a sigh of relief.

Cavalli smiled. "I got out of the corporate world so I wouldn't have to work so much, but here I am working just as much as ever. Who knew running a restaurant was hard?"

Tucker grinned. "When you're doing what you love, it isn't work."

"Ah, you speak the truth, my friend." Cavalli agreed.

Something inside me twisted at Tucker's words. I shied away from the feeling because it made me uncomfortable.

"I need to ask you something," Tucker said, his tone turning more serious.

"Of course," Cavalli replied, pulling over a chair from a nearby table and sitting down with us.

"It probably won't make sense, and I'm sorry, but I can't explain right now. I will when I'm able. But it's important."

"You know I will help you if I can."

I stared at Tucker. In that moment, he didn't just look like Max, but he sounded like him. Max was always so earnest when he spoke. He was always so straightforward. I admired that because I always knew what to expect.

Before Tucker continued his conversation, he gave me a small look, obviously noticing I was staring. I cleared my throat and took a sip of my water.

"Have I recently given you anything for safekeeping? A flash drive?"

To his credit, Cavalli didn't act as if the question was loony. He seemed to take it in stride and my heart began to pound in excitement. He must've known what we were asking about!

Justice is coming, Max.

Cavalli sat back in the chair and regarded Tucker for a long moment. "What's this about? Are you in trouble, Max?"

"I wish I could explain," Tucker said, sitting forward.

"No," he answered. "You haven't given me anything for safekeeping. I haven't seen you in weeks. Don't you remember?"

Tucker smiled. "Of course. I just need confirmation."

Cavalli sat forward. "Max, you know if you need help, I will be there."

Something shifted behind Tucker's eyes. Sorrow perhaps. And then it was gone. "You've been a great friend to… to me. Good friends are hard to come by these days and you've been one. Thank you."

He was thanking this man for being so good to his brother. For being there for him even when he wasn't. I felt the sting of tears behind my eyes and I pushed them back.

Tucker carried a lot of guilt inside him. For the men who died that he couldn't save. For his brother who he pushed away and now would never get to tell he was sorry…

I wondered what other pieces made up the man that Tucker was. I wanted to know them. I wanted to know everything I could about him. I realized I wasn't just wildly attracted to him. He didn't just make my pulse race… I liked him.

Cavalli smiled. "Nothing you wouldn't have done for me." He stood and clapped Max on the back. "Meal's on the house."

He planted a light kiss on my cheek and then went back to the kitchen.

We sat there in charged, disappointed silence.

"I wasn't here when he needed me most," Tucker said quietly.

"Well, I was here and didn't even know he was in trouble." I added.

"The flash drive's not here. We need to keep looking." He pushed away from the table and stood. After dropping a generous tip on the table, he walked away without looking to see if I would follow.

Sometimes his mood swings gave me whiplash.

I looked around the restaurant one final time, remembering the last time I was here. It was with Max. We came for dinner, we talked about work a lot, but we had some good laughs too. That dinner was the last date we'd ever have.

Tucker reappeared beside the table. I tilted my head back to look up at him. "You okay?"

I nodded, swallowing thickly.

"I'm sorry I was an ass."

I felt my lips pull up. "That was difficult for you, wasn't it?"

"What?"

"Apologizing."

"I usually prefer to deliver my apologies in a different way," he said suggestively. The desire that waved off his body literally melted me to the floor.

I didn't know how to respond. Most men I talked to, most men I interacted with, were not even half as sexual as Tucker was. It was like he thought about sex every three seconds.

Thankfully, I was saved by my ringing cell in my bag. I pulled it out, noting on the screen it was my mother. I would have let it go to voicemail, but I needed a way out of this conversation.

"Hi, Mom," I said, putting the phone up to my ear.

"Charlotte! How are you, honey?"

I stood from the table and followed Tucker across the polished floor toward the exit.

"I'm good, but I'm actually in the middle of something. Could I call you back in a bit?"

"Of course. I just wanted to tell you that I'm late mailing out your latest box." I almost groaned out loud thinking about the monthly box my mother always mailed me. The boxes I always had to go retrieve from the UPS store.

Wait.

The UPS store. The note left on my door.

"You haven't sent it yet?" I asked curiously.

"No, honey, and I'm sorry. But I found the cutest little slippers online. They will be just perfect for you on cold nights… but the color I wanted was all out of stock so I had to wait for them to come in. They arrived today so I will be mailing your box within a day or two."

Tucker held open the door to the outside and I stepped through, out onto the cold New York City sidewalk. If my mother hadn't sent me a package, then who did?

"Mom, I'm going to have to call you back," I said quickly, not waiting for her to say good-bye before disconnecting the call.

I spun, practically knocking into Tucker. "Whoa," he said, grabbing me by the shoulders. "Who was that?"

Was there anyone Max trusted—really trusted—that he might give it to for safekeeping? Tucker's question bounced around in my swirling mind.

I did know someone Max trusted.

Me.

My eyes collided with Tucker's. "I know where the flash drive is."

25

Tucker

"You really think it's in there?" I asked, standing in front of a UPS office, staring in the wide glass window at all the boxes and shipping supplies.

"If it isn't, then I'm out of ideas on where to look," Charlotte replied, rummaging around in her purse in search of some note the UPS left on the door of the apartment about a package just a few days ago.

I prayed to God it was in that package and that it had all the evidence the Feds would need to put away Wallace Jr. and Sr. and whoever else was guilty of corporate espionage and killing my brother.

"Got it!" she exclaimed, holding up a crumpled piece of paper.

We went inside and I practically paced the room while waiting for them to retrieve her package out of the back and hand it over. It was a small manila envelope addressed to Charlotte in neat handwriting. We both stared down at it like it held a ticking bomb.

After she signed for it, I wrapped an arm around her elbow and guided her over to the corner of the store, near a large counter where people could pack boxes. "Open it."

"Here?"

Hell yes, here. I couldn't wait another minute to see if it was what we'd been searching for. "Here's as good a place as any."

Charlotte tore the top off the envelope and turned it upside down. A small box and a folded piece of paper fell out onto the counter. I couldn't help but notice the way Charlie's hand trembled when she reached for the box. It was about the size of a jewelry box, a small rectangle. She lifted the lid and then overturned it in her palm. When she drew the bottom of the box away, I stared down…

At the black flash drive.

I felt a sadistic grin curve my mouth. *Got you, motherfuckers.*

Pride swelled within me when I thought of Max and his smart actions. The safest place for that drive was exactly where he put it. No one would think to look in the mail for it, as not many people mailed stuff to their own house.

Even if they had stormed this place, they likely wouldn't have found it because the delivery guy would have it on his truck every day for attempted delivery. Requiring Charlotte's signature was a stroke of genius because it guaranteed the package had to be placed directly in her hands.

You did good, brother. You did good.

"Oh, Max," Charlotte said, drawing me out of my thoughts. We were standing close, the side of her shoulder practically brushing against my chest. She tipped her head back and looked up at me, cradling the drive in her hand between us. "This seems like such an insignificant thing to die for."

Sorrow filled her hazel eyes and her lower lip trembled ever so slightly. I covered her hand with mine. "We'll make sure his death wasn't insignificant." I promised.

She sniffled and nodded. "What now?"

"Now I call the Feds and set up a meeting with them to hand over the drive. Hopefully whatever is on it will be enough to get warrants and make arrests. And then it will all be over."

I paused, using my fingers to deftly release her hair from the frigid style. It untwisted quickly, falling down her back. I tucked one of the waves behind her ear. "You'll be safe."

"And you'll go to North Carolina," she added softly. Was that some regret I heard in her tone?

"We should go," I said, picking up the empty envelope and turning to throw it in the trash just a couple feet away.

When I turned back, Charlotte was standing rigidly, with both the drive and the piece of paper that was with it clutched in her hands. Her gaze was locked on something outside the glass windows.

"Charlie?" I asked, going to her side, noting the way all the blood drained from her face, leaving her looking ashen and white. "Hey." I wrapped an arm around her shoulder, pulling her into my chest.

"It's him," she whispered.

"Who?" Alert caused my blood to surge, and for the first time I looked up to see what caused her to be rooted into place.

She wasn't staring at something, but *someone*.

"Garlic Breath," she whispered as a little tremble shook her body.

Not really understanding who this man was, but knowing it wasn't good, I looked back at the man Charlie referred to as Garlic Breath. His eyes were locked on her and his stare was cold and calculated.

He moved, causing his coat to shift, and I caught the unmistakable outline of a gun at his waist. "Is that the man who tried to kidnap you?" I whispered, noting he wasn't alone. Several of his "friends" were climbing out of a car parked at the curb.

She nodded.

I didn't really need her confirmation though because the second the words left my lips, the man boldly pulled out his gun and aimed it right at us. I knew the look of a man intent on hitting his mark. I knew the look of a man who wasn't afraid to shoot.

He had that look.

"Go!" I yelled, turning my body so it created a shield in front of Charlie as I pushed off the tile floor to sprint away from the window.

Behind us, the sharp sound of shattering glass penetrated the air. Thousands of jagged shards rained into the store as the bullet cut through the window like a hot knife through ice cream cake.

I shoved Charlie hard, pushing her onto the floor and covering her body with mine. Another bullet cut through the air as people screamed, horns honked, and chaos reigned. Little cuts stung my skin, but I forced the pain away, focusing instead on surviving.

Flashbacks from the war, flashbacks of the sound of my brothers screaming in death, and the sound of roaring flames took over my brain.

Not again.

A bullet tore into the tile, right beside us, far too close to home, and caused the floor to crack and explode, raining even more blunt objects our way.

I jumped up, practically picking Charlie up by the back of her shirt and shoving her roughly toward the back of the store. "Run!" I roared. "Get the hell out of here!"

She didn't have to be told twice and ran behind the counter, skidding across the rubble from the broken glass and catching herself before nearly wiping out. I wasn't far behind her, knowing that the men who were willing to cause such a scene in public weren't going to stop until we were dead and the drive was theirs.

The sound of a shotgun being cocked had me pausing. I turned as the man who had been working behind the counter drew himself up to his full height and took aim at the men attempting to kill us.

From this close, I could see the sweat beading his forehead and I knew he never thought he would have to use that gun. No one ever thinks they're going to have to use one.

He hesitated to pull the trigger.

Garlic Breath did not.

His bullet was true to its mark and within seconds embedded itself right in the center of the man's head. Blood splattered across the counter and sprayed the wall.

Charlotte screamed.

The shotgun fell from the man's grip as he crumpled to the floor.

I shoved Charlotte again, reminding her to move, and yanked the shotgun out of the dead man's hands. He wasn't going to need it anymore.

I fired off a shot as I worked my way into the back, unable to aim as we scrambled back but able to hold off our pursuers to buy us a much needed few seconds.

The sound of falling boxes caused me to turn in time to see Charlotte trip over a stack of mail and fall onto the floor.

"Get up," I ordered. "Find the backdoor!"

I heard her scramble up as the man who killed the mail guy came bursting around the corner after us.

I aimed and fired.

The bullet tore into his shoulder, ripping muscle from bone as blood scattered across his cheek. The impact of the shot threw him backward and he fell. The gun he was toting skidding across the floor and underneath a cabinet.

He gave a shout of pain and then like an injured animal, he began to struggle to get back to his feet.

A couple more men came around the corner, their attention diverted to their bleeding friend, and I took aim again.

"Tucker! Let's go!" Charlotte yelled, and I felt the stirring of cold air at my back. She must have found the door. The sound of guns being cocked told me that more than one man had us in his sights.

I kept the shotgun aimed and steady as I backed toward the cold air. When I got close enough, I felt Charlotte's hand on my shoulder as she yanked me through the exit and slammed the door.

I let out the breath I'd been holding and glanced at her.

There was blood on her face.

I grabbed her chin, pulling her around so I could ascertain how injured she was. Flashbacks of Connors lying in the sand, bleeding out and moaning filled my mind.

I shook my head. I didn't have time for that right now. Charlotte needed me.

"Where are you hurt?" I demanded, squeezing her chin.

"It's not my blood," she replied, her voice flat.

We were standing very close to the man who was gunned down right in front of us. I probably had some of his matter on my face as well.

A bang on the door behind us caused my body to tense, and I glanced up the alley, noting the traffic whizzing by at the end. "Let's go."

We took off running. The sound of our feet pounding against the pavement seemed far away compared to the thumping of blood in my ears.

The door to the UPS store banged against the brick when the men barreled through, giving a shout as they saw us running, and gave chase. A bullet hit the side of a building beside us and Charlotte screamed, reaching up to cover her head with her arms. I kept running, scooping her up as we went, and dragged her the rest of the way down the alley.

Another shot rang out and I practically threw Charlotte away from me and out onto a busy sidewalk.

I turned back and fired off another round, the shotgun casing making a hollow ping when it hit the ground. One of the men went down and I smiled.

But the smile was short lived.

Because Charlotte screamed.

Forgetting all about the men chasing us, I barreled out onto the sidewalk, looking wildly around. She wasn't hard to find.

Because she was the only one on the street with a gun to her head.

I stepped forward, holding my hands up in surrender. I wasn't quite ready to put down my gun because if I had an opportunity to shoot, I damn well would.

The man holding Charlotte was who she referred to as Garlic Breath. He was sweating profusely, pale, and bleeding openly from the hole I put in his shoulder.

Frankly, I was impressed he was still standing.

He pressed a black pistol right up against Charlotte's temple, and she was trying to shy away, but his other hand was gripping the back of her neck, pinning her in place. Some people gathered around, watching the unfolding horror. Other people were scurrying away. I kept my eyes directly on Charlotte and that gun as someone behind me whispered into their cell phone to who I hoped was the police.

I tried not to be distracted by Charlotte's terror-filled eyes. I tried not to be distracted by the way her skin was completely colorless. Her hands were wrapped around her middle and she clutched the drive and piece of paper against her.

"Let her go," I said, once again showing him I would surrender.

"Drop the gun," he ordered.

I hesitated. He yanked Charlotte's hair, making her cry out.

Slowly, I lowered the gun to the ground and laid it by my feet.

"Kick it away."

Gritting my teeth, I did as he asked, pissed that this was happening. I could barely think because fear coated my insides, slowly spreading like some kind of contagious disease. I'd seen men killed right in front of me. Men I considered my friends. It haunted me to this day, but I survived.

Something told me if I watched Charlotte die before me, I wouldn't survive it.

"Give it to me, bitch," the man growled in her ear.

She recoiled. "No."

He smacked her with the end of the gun, rocking her head on her shoulders. I leapt forward, and the gun turned on me.

I saw his finger on the trigger twitch.

"Here!" Charlotte cried, holding up the small black drive. "Take it!"

The distant sounds of sirens reached my ears. It was about damn time.

Garlic Breath ripped the drive out of her hand and then shoved her roughly to the ground. She fell on hands and knees, gasping for breath.

He leveled the gun at her back, a sadistic grin on his pallid face.

"No!" I roared as the bullet discharged, and I threw myself at her.

I plowed into her and the bullet plowed into me. Razor-sharp pain ricocheted through my entire body and I felt like someone had lit me on fire. With a deep grunt, I landed on top of her, crushing her against the pavement, wrapping my arms over her head to protect her further.

I felt blood begin to ooze out of my body, but I couldn't tell where I'd been hit. I hurt everywhere.

"Tucker!" Charlotte yelled, trying to wiggle out from beneath me, but I wouldn't let her.

"Hold still," I ordered as I reached for the shotgun lying just a few feet away. At the curb, a dark-colored sedan came to a screeching halt and the door opened. I saw one extremely polished black dress shoe step out onto the street.

The shotgun disappeared.

Hands reached for me, yanking me off Charlotte. She began to yell and I began to fight. Adrenaline helped me move; fear for Charlotte kept me upright.

I landed a couple punches to the men who were trying to pull Charlotte and me apart, and then someone pinned me from behind, holding my arms, twisting them behind my back. Another man, one of the men from the alley, approached holding a small device.

A taser.

I started to struggle anew, but it was no use.

He hit me in the center of my chest, sending sparks of hot electricity jolting through my body and making me twitch. I spun, falling toward the ground, but hands caught me.

The last thing I saw was Charlotte being forced into the back of the car, and the last thing I heard was her screaming my name.

26

Charlotte

They were just letting him bleed.

The red soaked his shirt, saturating the fabric of the white button-up he was wearing. His skin, which usually held a golden tone, was now pasty, and every time I looked at him, the stain was wider than before. It was an all too grim reminder that time wasn't on our side. If we didn't get out of here soon, he was going to die.

I can't lose them both.

The thought had me sitting up a little straighter. Max was gone, his life cut entirely too short. But Tucker was still here and he had come to mean a lot to me in such a short amount of time. I knew that we likely would go our separate ways and that was fine, but the thought of him not being out there at all… it hurt me.

"You got what you wanted. Please just let us go," I begged for like the fiftieth time since the men who took us hauled us into this abandoned building and tied our bodies to chairs.

I glanced at Tucker again, noting the way his chin lolled against his chest and how his breathing grew shallow. The way they harshly tied his hands behind his back only exaggerated the bleeding in his side, and I couldn't stop picturing the way the wound was being pulled farther open by his forced position.

"So you can run right to the cops? Ain't gonna happen," one of the men said from across the room.

There were four of them. They were all sitting around a table with a laptop in the center. I could see the flash drive I surrendered to keep Tucker from being shot lying beside it (Fat lot of good that did me). Also sitting on the table were various paper sacks of fast food. The greasy, heavy smell literally made me want to gag. I couldn't imagine how anyone could eat at a time like this.

I guess kidnapping and attempted murder was a real appetite stimulant for those guys.

I couldn't help but think of all the charges that could be brought against these men when they got caught. Harassment. Stalking. Destruction of property, kidnapping, attempted murder, and those were just for starters. Oh, how I would love to get them in court and nail their French-fry-eating, bad-breath, Tucker-shooting asses to the wall.

But in order to do that, we had to get out of here. Giving up on the idea these men were just going to cut the ropes that bound my wrists, I began to study our surroundings. I looked for all the exits and for anything that could be used as a potential weapon.

Unfortunately, my choices were limited.

This was some sort of abandoned building and it was fairly empty, aside from trash littering the ground here and there.

"Is it what the boss needs?" one of the thugs who kidnapped us said, drawing my attention. He was standing behind the man at the laptop, eating some kind of giant burger, and as I stared at him, a big glob of ketchup fell out of the sandwich and onto his chest.

Wasn't he a real picture of manners? I bet girls lined up around the block to take him home to Momma.

Not.

"It's still pulling up!" the guy behind the computer said.

I wondered what kind of evidence was on that drive. I wondered if it was the only copy Max had. My guess was yes. It was our one shot at getting justice.

I also wondered what they were going to do with us once they realized they had the evidence and we were no longer necessary.

From somewhere in the building, I heard a man scream a string of profanities. I recognized his voice as Garlic Breath, the man who broke into my apartment, the man who Tucker shot, and the man reciprocated and shot Tucker.

It sounded like he was in a lot of pain and whatever kind of first aid his ghetto friends were administering wasn't helping.

A gunshot pierced through the building.

Out of the corner of my eye, I saw Tucker's slack form stiffen, but I didn't look his way because I didn't want to draw attention to either of us.

The single popping sound bounced off the walls and faded away, leaving everything and everyone in silence. Garlic Breath was no longer screaming.

There was a sick feeling inside me that whispered he couldn't scream anymore because he was dead.

What kind of people killed off their own allies when they were injured? Sick ones. Seriously mentally unstable people.

And we were at their mercy.

The man behind the computer whistled low beneath his breath. I looked up, noting his face as he stared at the screen. "Now I know why he wanted this shit so bad."

Computer guy looked up at me. His eyes seemed to glow with the bright artificial light shining out of the computer. "You're dead."

I shivered.

A man stepped out of the shadows. He was wearing a three-piece suit, well cut and expensive-looking fabric. His tie was made of silk and his dress shoes were shined so not a speck of dirt covered them.

His face was lined and slightly craggy. His hair was graying.

His eyes met mine.

Recognition struck me like a lightning bolt. It was Mr. Wallace, the CEO of the company Max worked for. We'd been to countless charity dinners with this man. We'd visited his home for a holiday dinner. I shared a meal with this man. We exchanged small talk and he and Max joked about sports.

"Ms. Carter," Mr. Wallace Sr. inclined his head. "My apologies you became involved in this unfortunate situation."

Disgust rolled through me and threatened to rot my insides. I barked out a harsh laugh and strained against the binds. "Unfortunate?" I spat. "You disgusting little worm. How could you?"

He didn't seem offended by my insult. "It's business."

As if that somehow made everything he'd done okay.

"I hope you rot in hell," I spat.

"I very well might, Ms. Carter, but I daresay that you will get there long before me."

His cocky, haughty attitude made me so angry that all I could think about was clawing out his beady little eyes.

"Is it all there?" he asked the man controlling the computer.

In response, he turned the screen so Mr. Wallace could take a look at whatever was on the file. As he read, his face flushed with anger. "You've certainly been a busy boy, Max."

The man eating the ketchup-dropping burger looked at his boss and was given a light nod. My stomach cramped as he made his way across the room toward us. His eyes were intent on Tucker, and I wanted to cry.

"Hey, asshole," I taunted, trying to draw his attention away from Tucker. "You ever heard of a napkin? Or maybe a shower?"

Okay, yes, those were horrible insults, but it was all I had.

He gave me the finger.

His insult sucked too.

Tucker was still out of it, his head still down, his eyes closed. I was beginning to worry that he had slipped into a coma... or worse.

The man struck out quickly, slapping Tucker across the side of the head so hard that the sound of flesh hitting flesh made me scream.

"Stop it!" I wailed, struggling anew. The chair I was sitting in jostled around on the floor.

Tucker's head rolled back on his neck and then flopped forward again. The man grabbed the top of his head, taking in the short hair in his fist, and yanked his head back to stare down into his face.

"Wake up," he snarled.

When Tucker didn't comply, the man used his free hand to stick two fingers into the still-bleeding bullet wound.

Tucker screamed and surged up in the chair. His eyes flew wide and his teeth slammed together. Hot tears rolled down my cheek. Not because I was sad. Not because I had given up. Because I was so incredibly angry. I was so incensed that I was shaking. I wanted nothing more than to get out of this chair and attack every single asshole in this room. I had never been a violent person. In fact, I was always a firm believer in the law, but this...

This gave me a whole new outlook.

Some people didn't deserve jail. Some people didn't deserve a fair trial.

Some people just deserved to be shot and left to die.

If someone handed me a gun in that moment, I would not have hesitated to pull the trigger. I would empty the entire chamber out and look for more bullets.

"Where are the copies?" the man torturing Tucker demanded.

Tucker stared at him in stony silence.

The man shoved his face as close to Tucker's as he could. "Where. Are. They?" He spit when he talked. I could see the little bubbles spew from his mouth and land on Tucker's face. Then he shoved his fingers back into the bullet wound.

I whimpered and started wiggling around in my chair once more. I saw the pain cross over Tucker's face. I saw the little lines that formed on the corners of his eyes.

Yet he made not one sound.

And he didn't look away from the man hell-bent on getting him to talk.

The man shoved Tucker back, rocking the chair, and paced away, then came back and glared. "You're a lot tougher than I expected a businessman to be," he said.

Once more, Tucker said nothing.

Ketchup Man turned back to Mr. Wallace, who nodded.

"Please," I begged, just wanting them to stop. I couldn't sit here and watch him get beaten. I couldn't watch the body that gave mine so much pleasure being abused. I couldn't watch the eyes that stared into me so intently when he would enter me again and again tighten in pain.

Ketchup Man rolled his head on his shoulders like he was getting ready for some kind of sporting event. And then he drew back his meaty fist and swung it forward.

Just as the fist was about to meet its target, Tucker moved. His arms surged forward, coming around his body, and he caught the incoming fist in his right palm. I watched his hand close around the man's knuckles. I watched the bones of Tucker's fingers strain against his skin as he tightened his grip until it had to hurt.

The man who thought he had the upper hand grunted under the pain.

Keeping his grip, Tucker pushed up out of the chair, kicking it backward, sending it skittering across the floor and crashing into a nearby wall.

"I'm not a businessman," Tucker growled, twisting the man's arms until he fell onto his knees.

"I'm a Marine."

Everyone looked around in shock, like they had no idea what was going on.

The man at his mercy groaned and Tucker pulled back is fist and sucker punched him in the side of the head. He fell forward, coming onto his hands and knees, and Tucker took the opportunity to deliver a strong kick to his ribs.

I heard a cracking sound and Ketchup Man sprawled across the floor.

"And you tie shitty knots," Tucker added, bringing his left wrist up, which still had a length of rope wrapped around it. As he was unwrapping, the men at the table shot up and rushed him.

"Watch out!" I screamed as two men approached, but Tucker didn't need my warnings. He swiped the first man's feet out from under him, sending him falling on his ass, and then drove the heel of his shoe right down on the man's crotch.

The man rolled into the fetal position and began to vomit profusely.

"Some guys just don't deserve nuts," Tucker spat.

The other guy paled but still came at him so Tucker put him in a chokehold and then used the rope from around his wrist to create a garrote. The man gasped as his airway was being cut off, and Tucker stepped around his back, practically straddling him to apply even more pressure. The man's eyes began to bulge as he clawed at the crudely made weapon strangling him.

Had Tucker been faking this whole time? Had he really been awake but just didn't want anyone to know it?

He still looked like hell, with sweat creating a sheen across his skin, his shirt soaked with blood, and dark circles pronounced beneath this eyes, but even in his exhaustion, he wasn't about to give up.

Suddenly, I understood how he managed to walk ten miles in the dessert while carrying a wounded man.

Determination.

Drive.

And a hell of a dose of badass.

The man's struggles to get away began to wane and I knew he was just minutes from losing consciousness.

I was so intent on Tucker and what he was doing that I hadn't noticed Mr. Wallace Sr. approach me. Until he placed a gun to my head.

God. This was just not my day.

How many times could a girl be held at gunpoint before she went mad (or actually got shot)?

"If you want her to live, you better drop him," Wallace said calmly.

Tucker released his prey and the man fell to ground, wheezing and desperately sucking in air.

"You got a problem with me," Tucker said, "you come at me. You don't threaten a woman."

Geez, if I wasn't tied to this chair, I would show him women could be badass too.

"You don't threaten *my* woman," he added, his gaze meeting mine for just seconds.

Okay, this wasn't the time for romantic gestures, but that totally made my heart skip a beat. Maybe he was just acting. Maybe he was playing the part of Max. But Max had never called me his in the entire year we dated. Max had never taken a bullet for me either.

"If you had just died the night of the crash like you were supposed to, she never would have been involved," Wallace Sr. said.

Tucker took several steps toward us. The hand holding the gun to my head wavered. "Stay where you are."

"No."

I glanced at Tucker, wondering what the hell he was thinking. He was baiting a man who was holding a gun to my head.

Hell-O… that qualified as a *don't piss off the crazy man* moment.

"I'll shoot her!" he said, jamming the gun a little bit harder into my head.

"When I was in Iraq, I learned some interesting things," Tucker drawled. "Like how to sever a man's spine, leaving him paralyzed but still able to feel."

The gun against my head wobbled. Tucker took another step closer, prowling toward the man with a wild look in his focused eyes. If I didn't know him, I would be frightened. The contrast of his pale skin against his dark, red-rimmed eyes was creepy. Added to the fact that he had blood literally all over him, he looked like a walking corpse.

"Do you know the kinds of pain I could inflict and you would only be able to lay there and feel it?"

"You're lying," Wallace Sr. said. I could tell he was shaken.

"Oh, I can assure you I'm not," he replied. "And perhaps after I'm done using you as a live cadaver, I will put you in a car, drive you around at excessive speeds, and then crash it, leaving you to lie inside the crumpled metal while I douse the body in gasoline and then light it on fire. You won't be able to run. But you'll be able to feel the heat of the flames. You'll be able to hear the groaning of the metal as the fire stalks you. And then when you start to burn, it will not only feel like the worst pain of your entire life, but you will smell the melting of your flesh."

The picture that Tucker painted with those words would live in my nightmares for years to come.

"Who the hell are you?" Wallace Sr. whispered horror in his tone.

"I'm Max's other half," he growled.

And then he pounced.

27

Tucker

You know, I'm a laidback kind of guy. I like to drink beer, hang out with my buds, and take random girls home for casual sex (Yes, I use a condom; I'm not nasty). I'm slow to anger and even slower to put myself out there to care about anyone.

But when I get pissed. *I get pissed.*

And seeing Charlie with a gun to her head pissed me off.

She had to be the first person since high school to slip past my defenses and worm her way into my affection so damn fast. Not even Nathan had managed to become like family to me so quickly.

How the hell a bossy, uptight, schedule-oriented person like her could ever turn my head was completely beyond me.

But then I thought about her heart-shaped lips, her gold-fringed hazel eyes, and the little sounds she made whenever I put my lips upon her skin.

And her laugh… She had a really good laugh.

Being tasered was fuel to the fire, and as I sat tied to a chair, dripping blood all over the filthy concrete floor, and listening to Charlotte beg the men to let us go, I began to grow livid.

But even livid, I remained cool headed. The Marine Corps taught me a lot. Self-control, self-reliance, self-defense. It also taught me how to keep my mouth shut and use the element of surprise. Pretending to be unconscious, pretending to be weak… Well, that gave me an advantage.

It was also an advantage that these asswipes couldn't tie a knot to save their damn lives.

Being tied up and thrown into the bottom of a pool in training taught me how to get out of a knot fast. Real fast.

And yeah, I was weak from blood loss, twitchy from being tased, and royally fucking pissed off.

Oh, and the *bullet hole* in my side hurt like a bitch.

But it wasn't enough.

It wasn't enough to put me down. It wasn't enough to make me give up. We weren't dying here tonight. I wouldn't allow it.

And so I took my opening.

And now here I stood facing Mr. Wallace Sr.—some old guy on a power trip—and once again he was pissing me off by holding a gun to Charlie's head.

When I was done telling him exactly what I would do to him if he even tried to hurt her, I think he finally got the message.

The message I was not going to be fucked with.

"Who the hell are you?" he whispered.

Who was I he wanted to know. *Who was I?*

I was someone I hadn't wanted to admit to being for a long time. And that lack of admission would haunt me for the rest of my life.

I was done pushing that part of me away. Doing so had gotten me nothing but regret.

"I'm Max's other half."

I launched myself forward. Even shot, I was light on my feet. He pulled the gun away from Charlotte and aimed it at me, firing off a shot that went wild. I bulldozed into him, knocking him into the ground and landing on top of him. The gun was between us and he pointed at my chest.

I spit in his face, right in his eyes. Little bits of saliva mixed with blood shot into his eyes and he cursed, closing them, trying to clear his sight. With a flip of my wrists, I disarmed him, using the butt of the gun to strike him in the side of the head.

His body went slack beneath me.

Not willing to let my guard down, I kept the gun trained on his head as I stood, the wound in my side bleeding profusely and the world around me tilting.

Wallace was out cold.

Behind me Charlotte struggled, so I went to her, released the binds that held her, and she launched out of the chair and into my chest.

I groaned when she made contact, and she pulled back with a gasp. "Oh my God!" She freaked. "Tucker, we need to get you to a hospital!"

"I'll be fine, darlin'," I said, even though I felt like shit.

The man whose junk I stomped on groaned and rolled onto his back. His face was blotchy and he had puke on his shirt. He fumbled with the waistband of his pants and in two strides, I was at his side and disarming him of the gun he was so kindly going to try to kill me with.

"Thanks. I was almost out of bullets," I said.

He groaned and rolled back into the fetal position.

Charlotte ran to the computer and pulled out the flash drive. Her purse was lying in the corner of the room, all the contents spilled everywhere, and she went over to retrieve the bag, her wallet, and the paper that was with the drive. She left everything else there, forgotten.

Knowing that Wallace probably had a cell phone on him, I turned to search his coat.

One of his lackeys was standing over his body with a gun pointed directly at me.

"I'm really tired of this shit." I sighed wearily. "Drop the gun or I'll shoot your ass."

"I c-can't let you leave with that drive," he said, the gun shaking tremendously in his hand. He probably saw me drop everyone else in the room, and if my suspicions were correct, he was the one that probably put down the guy I shot with the shotgun. He probably hadn't planned to come out at all until he realized he was the last hope of Wallace keeping that drive.

He couldn't be more than nineteen years old. A kid who got caught up in something he didn't know how to get out of.

I didn't want to shoot him.

Didn't mean I wouldn't.

"Look, kid…" I tried to reason with him. "Put the gun down and get the hell out of here. I won't tell no one you were here. Let this be a lesson to you. You roll with idiots, you become an idiot."

He didn't lower the gun, but I saw the desire in his eyes. The desire to get the hell out of here.

"I'm only offering once."

He laid the gun down and took off running.

My gun followed him until he was out of sight.

On my way over to Wallace's body, I stumbled. The damn room was really spinning and it was getting darker in here.

"Tucker," Charlotte worried and appeared at my side, slipping her body beneath my arm and lending support.

"See if he has a phone. I gotta call the Feds." Our phones had been confiscated before we got here, and I had no idea where they were.

"Sit down," she demanded.

Sitting down seemed like a pretty good idea. I lowered myself down against the wall, at a vantage point that I could see the room and watch the men I knocked out. They wouldn't stay that way much longer. We were going to have to move. Soon.

The breath hissed between my teeth when I leaned against the wall. Charlotte stood and yanked the green shirt over her head. My eyes fixated on the peach lace cups that supported her perky tits.

What? I was shot, not dead.

The way her creamy flesh practically spilled out of the tops of the cups made my mouth salivate.

'Course this really wasn't the time for a quickie.

"What the hell are you doing?" I asked her.

She kneeled down and pressed the shirt to my wound.

"Shit!" I cursed.

"Don't be a baby," she scolded, pressing harder.

Don't be a baby she says. "I have a bullet embedded in my side and you're pushing on it."

"We need to stop the bleeding," she said. "Push!"

I placed my hands over hers and added some pressure.

Her hands felt warm. It was nice. "You know," I said, leaning my head against the wall, "in a movie, it's usually it's the guy who takes off his shirt to stop the bleeding of his girl."

The side of her lip curled up. "Good thing this isn't a movie."

"If it was, you'd be my girl," I said, tugging on the end of her hair.

Clearly I was becoming delirious from loss of blood, likely shock and too much adrenaline pumping through my system. I was starting to spout those pretty words I didn't know how to say.

"Please don't die," she whispered, her voice cracking.

"Die?" I scoffed. "This is nothing. Did I ever tell you I walked ten miles carrying a guy who was shot?"

She nodded. "Yeah, you told me."

"Did I tell you I had been shot too?"

Her eyes widened. "No."

I smiled. "Takes a lot more than a bullet to kill me, darlin'."

Charlotte's palm was warm when she cupped my cheek and smiled.

"I need that phone."

There was a black phone in the inside pocket of Wallace's jacket, and she spun, holding it up triumphantly. I grinned and tried to remember the number the Feds gave me.

Charlotte shrieked.

I opened my eyes. Wallace was awake and had his hand wrapped around her ankle, trying to pull her feet out from under her.

I lifted the gun and shot him. He yelped and let go, rolling onto his bleeding arm.

The side door to the building burst in and people began swarming the room. I launched up off the floor, holding out both my guns, and put myself in front of Charlotte.

"Freeze!" a deep voice yelled, pointing a gun at me.

It was the cops. It was about fucking time.

One of the *Men in Black* came through the door, weaving around all the men dressed in black with the word SWAT across the back of their jackets.

"They're with us," he called, motioning toward me and Charlotte.

"What took you so long?" I barked as he approached.

"We need the medics!" he yelled, and people went off to do his bidding. "Did you get the drive?" he asked.

"Yeah. Yeah, we got it."

Charlotte handed him the drive out of her bag. He slipped it into a clear bag labeled *evidence*. Everyone in the room was looking at us and I was starting to feel like the big man on campus until I realized they weren't looking at me.

Charlotte was standing around in her bra, giving every man in here a show.

"Hey," I said to the man in black.

"It's Carson," he said, giving me a name.

"Carson, you mind giving my girl here your jacket?"

He chuckled and draped it around her shoulders.

"Keep that shit covered up," I told her as the medics rushed into the room, surrounding me with their tools.

She moved aside, giving them space to work, but I kept my eyes on her. Even when the room began to spin and my eyes grew heavy, I didn't look away.

Shouting filled the distance and commotion erupted around me; people crowded in and blocked my view. I heard her call my name… I tried to answer…

Shadows descended, cloaking me in solitude, and then there was no more.

28

Charlotte

The sound of white sneakers squeaking over a polished floor reverberated out in the hallway. The room was dim, but the florescent light just outside the door made it difficult to sleep. Well, that and the fact I was sitting in the most uncomfortable chair known to man.

Every time I closed my eyes and attempted sleep, I heard the sound of gunfire and felt Tucker jerk against me as the bullet meant for me ripped into his side. After a while of struggling to sleep, I gave up, instead leaning back in the chair and watching him sleep.

He seemed comfortable. The medicine the doctors gave him kept the pain at bay. As he slept, I took advantage of the fact he was out and studied his face.

It's funny because I would have thought that looking at his square jaw, dark hair, and straight nose would be like a sucker punch every time I gazed his way. I thought he might be a constant reminder of

Max, that being near him would hurt and cause more grief than I already felt.

But it wasn't like that at all.

Yes, he looked just like Max. However, when I looked at him, all I saw was Tucker. He was a distinct man, an unreplicated version of himself.

When I thought of Max, I smiled. I felt pride we had been together. We made a great team. Together we were unstoppable. There would forever be a piece of me that missed him, a piece in my heart reserved just for him.

When I thought of Tucker…

When I thought of him, heat swam through my middle. Passion like I'd never known before took over my body and caused my hands to ache to touch him. With him, everything seemed unpredictable; everything was unscripted. It wasn't nearly as scary as I thought those feelings might be. If anything, they made me feel alive.

All those feelings were good… yet they made me feel incredibly guilty.

Guilty that I hadn't felt that way for Max. Guilty that my first thought when I learned Max was gone was that I lost my friend. Shouldn't I have felt more? Watching Tucker succumb to his wound last night scared me to my bones. The unrelenting fear of him dying still left my stomach achy and weak.

Unknowingly, I told Tucker I liked him better.

It was true.

And for that I would never forgive myself.

Slight movement on the bed caught my eye, and I sat up, pushing forward. Tucker blinked, his eyes opening slowly as he stared around the room.

"You're at the hospital, Tucker. You were shot."

He turned his head, spearing me with those endless dark eyes. "Hey," he rasped, his voice slightly hoarse. He smiled and it tilted my universe.

"Should I get the nurse?"

"You know what they say is the best medicine for healing a wounded man?" he asked.

"What?" I replied, knowing that whatever he asked for I would make sure he got.

"Human contact."

That was not what I was expecting to hear.

"Come here," he coerced, pulling his hand from beneath the cover and extending it to me.

I couldn't deny a man who almost died for me. I pushed out of the torturous chair and stepped to the side of the bed. He slid over, grimacing a little when he moved. I bit my lip, thinking I needed to call the nurse.

"I'm fine." He promised and held out his arm.

As carefully as I could, I slid onto the bed, stretching out alongside him, my cramped, sore muscles giving a great sigh of relief. He wrapped his arm around me and pulled me closer so the only place to rest my cheek was on his chest.

"You're cold," he murmured against my hair.

"I put the blanket they gave me over you."

I felt his lips move in my hair and my eyes fluttered closed. "Is this okay?" I asked, not wanting to hurt him.

"Perfect," he whispered.

"Thank you," I said, twisting my fingers in the side of his hospital gown. "For protecting me. I wish I'd done a better job at protecting you."

His breathing was even and deep, making me think he'd once again slipped into sleep. A few long moments passed as his heat seeped into my chilled skin and my cheek pillowed itself against his chest.

"Taking a bullet was easy," he said. "You have the hard job."

I didn't understand what he meant. Maybe he was confused from all the meds. "My job isn't hard."

"Darlin'," he drawled sleepily, "I can guarantee you that being the keeper of my heart is most definitely not going to be easy."

My breath caught. My entire body went numb. Did he just tell me I had his heart?

I pushed up to stare down at his face.

His eyes were closed and a light snore rose from his mouth. He was asleep. I lowered myself back against him, careful not to bump any of the wires and tubes.

He probably wouldn't remember what he said.

But me… I was never going to forget.

29

Tucker

Underlying tension.

It simmered beneath the surface like a bubbling pot threatening to boil over at any given moment.

For almost two weeks, I was able to ignore it. We were both able to pretend it wasn't there. But as the wound in my side healed and the sharp ache throbbing in my chest after Max's memorial service became just a little more bearable, the tension was a lot harder to ignore.

I was still in New York City, first because the doctors told me not to travel while my wound was still fresh and then because the FBI kindly asked me to stay while they built a solid case against Wallace and his band of criminals.

Charlotte stayed with me until I was released from the hospital. She never left my side, even when I tried to order her away. She insisted that I stay at her apartment, and I didn't argue because honestly, I wanted to be there. Charlie and I went through something together, something most people never do.

We were also both grieving over my brother, grieving over the person we both loved and lost. The memorial service was held here in the city, and the cathedral was so packed people had to stand. I wished Max could see the amount of people that came out to honor his short life. My parents stayed for several days, my mother cried a lot, and my father constantly shook his head.

Charlotte went back to work and my mother hovered in the apartment, constantly checking my wound like it was going to somehow open up and swallow me whole. But I didn't complain. Making sure her only living son wasn't going anywhere was part of her healing process. I knew this had been a shock to them. No one ever expected Max to be the one to go so young. If anything, my family always prepared themselves for my untimely death. Considering my old profession, it hadn't been farfetched.

But as the days crawled by, my mother began to realize that I wasn't going to die and my father finally convinced her to go back home.

The apartment was quiet during the day, and I spent a lot of time looking through Max's things, remembering my brother and regretting all the time we lost.

I hoped wherever he was, he knew how much he meant to me.

Nathan and Honor flew in for the service. Actually, they flew in when I told them I was in the hospital and they stayed until after the service. It was good to see them again. They had become my family, and I realized that nothing in life would ever be as important as that.

I was finally ready to stop pushing so many people away. I was ready to take on those relationships, to embrace them, because life was too short to have regrets.

Nathan knew how I felt the minute he saw Charlotte and me together. I never told him and he never came out and asked. But he knew. Right before he and Honor flew back to North Carolina, he came to the apartment and without my asking, he gave me some advice.

"Tuck," he said, "don't beat yourself up too bad about the way you feel. Max wouldn't want that. If anything, he'd want you to be the one to take care of her."

"That's the thing," I told him. "I don't feel the way I do out of obligation. I feel it because it's real."

Nathan smiled. "You know the PI firm sure could use a lawyer on staff to keep you and me on the up and up."

The suggestion settled inside me; it brought me a feeling of peace. Having Charlotte with me all the time just felt right.

Right before he left that day, he gave me a very manly hug. "Love is never a mistake, my brother. Don't let who she was with in the past keep you apart in the future," he said into my ear. "See ya at home."

I didn't love Charlotte. Not yet. I wouldn't let myself. But I knew when—*if*—I ever lowered those walls within me, even just a little, that loving her would be the easiest thing I ever did.

I didn't bring up Nathan's suggestion to Charlotte because I knew how she would react. She was back to pulling long hours at work, getting up and working out in the early morning hours, and while I knew she wanted me here, I couldn't help but notice how she went out of her way to avoid my touch.

I might be able to get past that she used to be my brother's, but I wasn't sure she ever could.

I understood it.

And now it was time for me to move on. For me to go home.

The key in the door was a distinct sound, and I glanced over from my position on the couch, watching Charlotte let herself in.

She was wearing a no-nonsense suit, heels, and her hair was severely brushed back from her face. The exhaustion in her face was clear and so was her unhappiness.

"Hey," I called.

"Hey." She dumped her briefcase and bag on the island and stepped up beside the couch. "How did your appointment go today?"

"Doc gave me a clean bill of health."

"Oh," she said, not sounding as happy as I expected. "That's wonderful."

"Yep," I said, deciding to test the waters. "He said I was okay to travel. So that means I can go to North Carolina."

"You're leaving?" she asked, her voice mildly alarmed yet resigned.

And that's when I knew.

I knew I couldn't walk out of here without at least trying. I wanted her too badly and I hoped she wanted me too.

"Nathan can't do all the work at the PI firm forever."

"I suppose you're right," she said, backtracking into the kitchen.

Backtracking = running away.

A few cabinets opened and closed, and I heard some liquid being poured into a glass. I stood and glanced at her. She was pouring a glass of wine.

I stifled a grin.

"What are you doing home so early?" I asked, noting it was only early afternoon.

"I wanted to see how your appointment went." She took a sip of wine. "And now I know." Another swallow of liquor made it down her throat.

"I'm sure you'll be glad to get me off the couch and have the bathroom to yourself."

Charlotte grabbed the glass of wine and spun, putting her back to me. "You do snore."

I laughed.

When she kept her back toward me, I knew she was upset.

"Come with me," I said.

She stiffened and spun, clutching the glass in front of her. "What?"

"Come to North Carolina with me. The firm needs a good lawyer to keep me out of trouble."

The longing in her eyes practically stopped my heart. Damn. I knew she felt something for me, but I was always afraid that it hadn't been as strong as what I was feeling.

I was wrong.

The sheen of tears coated her eyes, making them sparkle against the afternoon sun filtering through the kitchen window. "I can't," she said, her voice catching.

Charlotte spun away again, turning so I couldn't see her face. The apartment grew still and quiet. Neither of us moved.

I asked. She answered. I should have walked away before it got any harder.

Fuck. That.

"There's more to living than just being alive," I said softly. My voice was like the pin drop you could hear in a silent room.

Her breath hitched and I knew I had a captive audience.

"There's more than just going through the motions of daily life." I took a step forward.

When I moved, she looked over her shoulder, our eyes colliding. It was as if we were tethered together, tethered by the words that rushed softly out of my mouth.

"More than putting on a suit and sitting behind a desk for eighty hours a week. More than scheduling time for everything from eating to brushing your teeth." The distance between us closed with every step I took, and it was like there was this invisible pull—this gravity that was pulling me toward her.

She swallowed thickly. I felt the movement more than I saw it. I knew how she felt. I knew exactly what her insides felt like.

It was the feeling you got just stepping off a tilt-a-whirl that spun you in erratic and random circles. It was the feeling that you experienced when you got shocked by something charged. Little sizzles of electricity raced just beneath the skin, causing everything to vibrate, everything to hum.

I knew that's what she was feeling...

Because I felt it too.

I stepped up close and her body swayed toward me, like fighting the pull between us was proving too hard. "I know you want to make your father proud," I said, reaching out to release her hair. "You want to follow in his footsteps, but he wouldn't want that for you. He wouldn't want you working so much and so hard that you have a fatal heart attack."

The clip slid out of her hair effortlessly, and I let it fall from my fingers onto the floor. Cascades of thick honey-colored hair waved out, falling down her back.

I grasped her by the shoulders and guided her around so I could delve not one, but both of my hands into the thick mass and pull my fingers through the silky waves, spreading it out over her shoulders.

"You're too beautiful for this," I whispered, tugging on the very tips of the strands. Her breathing caught when my knuckle grazed over her breast. "You're too beautiful to spend your life closed off from everyone, doing only the things you've made a list to do and refusing to veer from that path."

Leaning forward, I pressed a kiss to the corner of her lips, just enough to tease the fullness of her mouth, but not enough for complete contact. When I brushed against her again, I tasted the damp saltiness of a tear. I cupped her face, tilting her head back, and looked into her eyes. Single, silent tears were falling over her lashes and melting into my skin.

"Come with me, Charlie. Take a chance on life. Take a chance on me. I'll make you happy."

I captured her lips. I held her face firmly in my grasp and ravaged her mouth. I poured everything I had into that kiss, teasing and tasting. Taunting and giving. Her lips were a buffet and I planned to stuff myself until I was full.

Charlotte wrapped her hands around my wrists and squeezed, pressing just a little bit closer, applying a bit more pressure against our lips. Her tongue traced the outline of my lower lip, and she sucked it into her mouth, making me groan. I tilted my head in the opposite direction and kissed her that way, and I stroked her with my tongue.

But it wasn't enough.

Roughly, I pulled her head back to give me better access, and I swept my tongue inside her mouth, releasing her face and letting my hands roam over her body. I didn't bother with the buttons on the front of her blazer, instead ripping it open. The sound of skittering buttons floated across the floor.

Charlotte's chest heaved and her swollen breasts pushed against my chest as I ripped away the jacket and tossed it aside.

Sliding my hands around the curve of her waist, I reached down, gripping her ass, and squeezed, tilting her pelvis so it came into contact with the hard rod in my pants.

She groaned and I thrust up against her, pushing her back against the counter and dry humping her right there through our clothes.

My lips slid down her neck, sinking lower, until I was able to close my mouth around her rigid nipple piercing through her clothes. She cried out when I clamped down around it, the dampness of my mouth soaking through her clothes and leaving a ring of desire on her chest.

Her fingers threaded through my hair, squeezing my scalp and urging me on, urging me for more.

I abandoned her breast and crouched down, gently running my hands up her calves, behind her knees, to roughly yank the tight knit skirt up around her hips. Excitement pounded through my veins and my hands shook with a fine tremor. It wasn't secret that I liked sex, but this…

This went beyond excitement.

Her butt hit the counter when I lifted her up and guided her down, pushing her thighs apart with my hips and stepping in between.

She was too far back for the kind of contact I wanted so I grabbed her knees and pulled, yanking her crotch right into my throbbing and anxious dick. She cried out and her head fell back, spilling long waves of hair over my hands where I kneaded her waist.

I snatched her hand and boldly placed it between us, rubbing it along my hard length. "Can you feel how much I want you? One night wasn't enough, Charlie. I want more."

Her little hand wrapped around the head of my cock and squeezed. My eyes rolled back in my head. "More," I whispered.

She squeezed again, and my penis jumped, straining against the jeans keeping it contained.

"Tell me you want me," I demanded, pulling back and looking into her heat-glazed eyes.

"I want you." She obeyed.

Our lips collided again, burning against each other, creating little sparks that shot off into the air around us, creating an electric charge in the room. I went for the buttons on her shirt. I wanted to be naked and inside her. *Now.*

"Wait," she said, but I was too far gone to hear her.

She yanked her lips away, leaning back against the cabinet. The sounds of her breathing were fast and hard. "Tucker, wait," she said again, more forceful this time, placing a hand against my shoulder and stopping me from scooping her close again.

"I can't do this," she gasped.

"Yes, you can." I reached for her again.

"No." Charlotte pressed her lips together and looked at me with pleading eyes. "I can't do it to him. To Max."

"We already did," I argued, thinking back to the sex-filled night we shared.

"I can live with a momentary lapse in judgment, but this… We're talking about—" Her voice stalled.

"Forever," I finished. "We're talking about forever because you and I both know the pull between us is never going to go away."

"I know," she said, hollow. "But, I just… I can't."

Anger burned through me, at myself, my brother, and at her. "Tell me what you felt for him is stronger than what you feel for me."

She squeezed her eyes shut and shook her head. I grabbed her by the shoulders. "Tell me, Charlotte. Tell me that the passion burned so hot between you two that it scorched your skin. Tell me that he took you up against the bathroom wall and then again on the floor. Tell me that you screamed his name the way you screamed for me. Tell me you didn't schedule sex with him one day a week, like it was one more thing to cross off your to-do list."

She gasped and her eyes sprang open. "Saturday," she whispered. I wasn't sure if she was shocked or not that I figured it out.

"Can you tell me any of that?" I demanded, taking her chin in my grip and forcing her to look into my face.

"No."

"Then… why?" *Why won't you take a chance on me?*

"He was my best friend. I can't betray him. Not even his memory."

I heard the finality in her tone, the decision. I shoved away from the counter, my fist balled tight, and all I wanted to do was hit something. She was choosing my dead brother over me.

It hurt like hell.

Expelling a deep breath into the room, I walked away, into the bedroom, where I reached in the closet and pulled out my leather jacket. A quick glance around told me I owned nothing else here; there was nothing for me to even pack.

Everything in this house belonged to Max. Including the woman with my heart.

She was still sitting on the counter when I stepped back into the room. I remained on the opposite side of the island, keeping it between us as some sort of defense.

"I'm not going to push you. You've been through enough."

"Tucker," she said, a single tear rolling down her cheek.

"There isn't anything left for me here, so I'm going home." I wasn't about to drag this out any more than I had too. That wasn't my style.

I took one last look at her, then turned and walked away.

She let me go.

30

Charlotte

I let him go.

I saw the veiled hurt in his eyes, and still I let him leave.

As soon as the front door shut, I burst into tears. Big, fat, ugly sobs ripped from somewhere deep inside my chest. I felt hollow, utterly empty.

The last two weeks had been a blessing and a curse. A blessing because Tucker had stayed. He let me take care of him, and having him here was like coming home to a surprise party. I just never knew what was going to happen.

One night I found him making pizza in the kitchen. Flour was everywhere, the cupboards were splattered with sauce, and cheese was all over the floor. The oven was smoking, and I'm not sure how it happened, but the pizza was still raw.

We ordered in that night.

Dominoes tasted better than Tucker's pizza.

A few days after that, when I came home he was in the shower… singing. His voice touched a part of my soul I never knew existed. Every word, every melody that came out of his mouth moved me in some small way.

At night, I would lie in bed alone, longing to get up and go to him, wanting so badly for him to quench my thirst for his body. Sometimes he would snore so loudly that I would lie there and giggle because he sounded like a lawnmower.

And now he was gone.

There would be no more messes in the kitchen. No more singing that reached my soul. No more giggles.

My body would still want him. My body would crave him until I died. It was a bold statement, but I knew it was true because he was the first man who ever taught me about passion, about the kind of pleasure a man could evoke from a woman.

But even still, I couldn't bring myself to betray Max like that.

How could I move on, living a life that made me insanely happy, when I realized that my life with Max had been anything but?

And to make it worse, the man who seemed to be able to give me the happiness that Max never could was his own brother, his other half.

Wiping the flowing tears off my cheeks, I jumped down off the counter, my knees threatening to buckle beneath me. With another sob racking my body, I flung myself across the couch, feeling as if the pain was going to rip me in two.

I wished Max was here. I needed my best friend.

I remembered the letter. The folded single piece of paper that was in the envelope with the flash drive he mailed me. I shoved off the couch and hurried into the bedroom, where I put it in a drawer when I was getting clothes to take to the hospital when Tucker was there.

I couldn't believe I forgot about it until now.

My hand closed around the paper and I sat down on the edge of the bed, wiping away another tear. I unfolded the wrinkled paper and looked down.

It was a letter. Written by hand, by Max.

Tears welled anew, just looking down at the last thing he would ever tell me. Looking at the last words I would ever know from him.

With a sniffle, I focused. And I began to read:

Charlotte,

If you're reading this, then I'm likely dead. I'm sorry I never told you, but I was approached by the FBI to gather evidence against Wallace (Jr. and Sr.) for corporate espionage. They aren't the only ones guilty within the company, but they are the main players. I found the evidence the Feds need, Charlotte. And now my life is in danger.

Please forgive me for never telling you about this. I did it for your protection. If you had known, they would be after you too.

Unfortunately, I must send you this because I'm afraid I won't be able to deliver it myself. I trust you more than anyone else in this town, and I know you will make sure these men are brought to justice.

Give this flash drive to Agent Carson of the FBI. He will know what to do.

Also, I'm sending for Tucker, my twin. If there is anyone that can keep you safe until you can deliver it, it's him. You can trust him. He's the best man I know. You're going to like him. He's exactly the kind of guy you need. He's the yin to your yang. The sugar to your coffee. Please tell him that even though we drifted apart over the years, he will always be my other half. My better half.

You and I… we're very similar, aren't we? It was easy to be together because we never challenged the other. We coexisted, but we never really united as a couple.

I'm not saying this to hurt you. I love you. I always will. I'm telling you this because I want you to have more in your life. The light in your eyes fades a little bit more every day, Charlotte. Now that I am faced with death, I realize that there is so much more to life than work. My time might be over, but yours, yours can just be beginning.

Use my death as a catalyst, a catalyst for great change, great happiness. For then, my death will serve a greater purpose.

You're my best friend, Charlotte. I want you to be happy. When you find love—when you find the man who makes you feel alive, grab hold of him and don't let go.

I love you always,
Max

The letter fell from my grasp and drifted to the floor. How horrible it must have been for him to think he was going to die. Yet Max approached it the same way he did everything else: with direct and methodical planning.

My heart hurt for him; my entire chest physically throbbed.

Beneath all the pain and sorrow, under the tears and guilt, I realized something else from Max's letter. He felt the same way I did. He realized we didn't have an epic love story; he realized we were more like best friends than anything else.

And he had been right.

We did coexist. We were like roommates who shared a bed, business partners who collaborated at home. And there was nothing wrong with that. It worked for us. We were something to each other that no one had ever been: best friends.

And in the face of his death, Max knew he had to tell me. He understood that I would be loyal to him even if it meant being alone.

He's the yin to your yang. The sugar in your coffee.

Max knew I would fall for Tucker. He approved.

A huge weight lifted off me just then, relieving me of my guilt and regret. Loving Max didn't mean pushing Tucker away, just as loving Tucker didn't mean not loving Max.

I had a feeling that the love I developed for Tucker would be as different as the love I felt for Max as the brothers were in personality.

I let him leave.

I let my future walk out that door. I turned him away.

I gasped and bolted off the bed, rushing through the apartment for the front door. Maybe he was still outside. Maybe he hadn't gotten a cab yet.

Maybe I could still catch him.

The door bounced off the wall when I flung it open and I barreled into the hallway, barefoot and all. "Tucker!" I yelled, knowing he couldn't hear me from outside but unable to keep his name from erupting from my chest.

Someone moved in the hallway and I gasped, stumbling backward.

Tucker pushed away from the wall he had been leaning against and faced me. "I was beginning to think you weren't coming."

A strangled sound somewhere between a moan and a laugh escaped me. I ran to him, racing across the carpet, and smashed into his chest. He chuckled as my arms wound around him beneath the leather jacket he was wearing and my fingers linked behind his back.

"Careful, darlin'," he grunted, and I gentled my hold around the area that was still healing.

"I never should have let you leave." I sobbed against his chest.

"I know."

"I thought I was betraying Max." I buried my face in the soft leather and inhaled. He smelled incredible.

"I know."

I laughed. "Is there anything you don't know?"

He bent, hooking an arm beneath my legs and swinging me up into his arms. "Yeah, I don't know why we're still standing out here."

In a few great strides, we were in the apartment, with Tucker kicking the door shut behind us. Setting me on my feet, his eyes took on a heated stare and my insides trembled because I knew what was coming.

He backed me up so I was pinned between him and the door. The buttons on my dress shirt gave way with one strong tug and they went flying in all directions. Once the shirt was fully off my body, he bent his head and sucked my nipple into his mouth, wetting the lacey fabric and using the rough texture to further spur my arousal. As he licked and sucked, his hands wound around my back and unhooked the clasp, releasing the cups completely.

"I want you naked," he growled. "I want absolutely nothing between us."

The bra was tossed aside and he reached for the zipper on my skirt, peeling it off my body, taking my panties away at the same time. When I was utterly bare, he took a step back and torched me with his heavy-lidded stare.

In seconds he pounced on me, pinning me once more to the door, and pressed his palm against the slick heat of my crotch, cupping the private space and sliding a finger right into my already aching insides.

But then he pulled away.

Breathing heavy and squirming with need, I watched as Tucker slowly undressed. He started with his jacket, sliding the leather off his body. His shirt was next, and I couldn't help but stare at the toned, cut muscles that made up his torso.

Staring at him was one thing, but touching that was something else.

He reached for the belt on his jeans and I dropped to my knees before him. As he undid the leather, I wrapped my mouth around his enlarged cock, letting my hot breath fan over his jeans.

He groaned and a shiver worked its way up his spine. I lapped at him through his jeans, enjoying the sounds of pleasure that erupted from his throat.

Soon he had the belt and button of his jeans undone, and I slid my fingers in the waistband and yanked down.

He wasn't wearing underwear.

Not able to wait until the jeans were all the way off, I dove forward, sliding my mouth all the way down the length of his penis. The skin was like taut satin stretched over an unrelenting rod. The juices inside me loosened and gushed forward, coating the insides of my thighs.

Tucker grabbed me by the hair and pulled me back, away from him, and kicked away the rest of his clothes. And now there was nothing between us.

No regret. No guilt. No clothes.

"Tucker," I moaned, wrapping my hands around the back of his neck and pulling his face down for a hungry kiss.

His strong hands wrapped around my hips and lifted. Before my legs were even locked around his waist, he surged inside me, so deep that I cried out.

Holding me close, he walked a few steps to the area rug where he kicked the coffee table out of the way and dropped to his knees. My body was shuddering around him. He felt so delicious that my body was ready to release on contact.

"Not yet, sweetheart," he purred, laying me out across the carpet but keeping us joined together. Supporting himself on his elbows, he looked down, pulling his fingers through my hair.

"Are you ready?"

"Please," I begged, lifting my hips, begging him to move. His cock jerked inside me, scraping against my inner walls and making me moan. My back arched off the floor and his lips closed around my nipple, sucking deep, sending sparks of pleasure shooting from my chest all the way down into the center of my body.

He surged forward, crashing our pelvises together, and created pressure on the already swollen button in between my folds.

"Cum for me, sweetheart," he said, lifting his mouth from my breast.

I splintered apart from the inside. Fragments of myself bounced around within the shell of my body, exploding into a surge of pleasure so great that my mouth fell open, yet no sound came out.

I couldn't speak. I could scarcely breathe.

He began to pump within me, surging in and out, sliding the incredible length of his rock-hard cock into my body again and again.

I couldn't do anything but lie there and let onslaught after onslaught of intense pleasure roll over my body.

And then he pulled out. It was so abrupt and so sudden I cried out. I reached for him, trying to drag him back. I wanted him inside me. I wanted to feel his desire.

"Charlotte, look at me," he commanded.

I opened my eyes and found his.

"Are you ready?"

"Yesss," I hissed, impatient. I already answered this question before.

He shook his head and leveled his body so it was brushing over mine and his penis was probing against my entrance, promising more pleasure.

"Are. You. Ready?"

"For what?" I cried, trying to push him into me. He pulled back, giving me a sly grin.

"For forever. Are you ready for forever?"

My eyes flew open. He was asking me to be his. Always. I didn't even have to think the answer. I knew it. I felt it.

"Yes," I whispered. "Yes."

He growled and pounded into me, wrapping his arm around my waist and anchoring our bodies together as he shouted his release. The joy of feeling his seed spill inside me was like nothing I'd ever known.

When our bodies stopped shaking, he rolled, bringing me with him, draping my satiated body across his chest.

"Tucker?" I whispered.

"Hmm?"

"Thank you for not leaving."

"I knew you'd come to your senses."

I propped my chin on his chest. "How did you know?"

His grin was lopsided. "Because I'm irresistible."

Well, I certainly couldn't argue with that.

EPILOGUE

Tucker

Later that year…

Ocean waves lapped against the shoreline of Topsail Beach, North Carolina. I tipped the longneck back to my lips, expecting the cool rush of beer to tantalize my mouth.

The bottle was empty.

I looked up at the house towering over the sand and wondered where the hell Nathan was with our beer.

It was a beautiful summer day, breezy and not too hot. People roamed the shoreline looking for shells and tossing Frisbees for their dogs. Usually at this time of day, Nathan and I were behind our desks, working on cases.

The PI business was a success. Our contacts with the Marines and our professionalism to get the job done made us the go-to guys for just about every kind of investigative service that was needed.

Just yesterday we signed a big contract with the Corps for a deal that was going to keep us busy for years to come. All the money Charlotte negotiated was a nice bonus too.

It was why we decided to take the day off, to enjoy the spoils of our riches. Well, that and the fact that Honor and Nathan had a sweet beach house right on the sand.

Now that the deal was signed, Charlotte and I planned to build one right next to them. Thoughts of Charlie warmed my blood, and I got the familiar rush of happiness and craving I also felt when I thought of her. She was the best thing that ever happened to me. A fact Honor reminded me about every single day.

Not that I needed reminding.

A shadow fell across the sand and I smiled. "About damn time. Did you have to go to the store for the beer?" I said, looking up at Nathan.

"I asked Nathan to stay up at the house with Honor for a couple minutes," Charlie said, holding the blowing hair back from her face.

Damn, she was gorgeous. Long, tan legs, tangled, golden hair, and eyes that were like a siren to my lost ship.

"Hey, darlin'," I drawled, patting the sand beside me. "Did you have fun shopping with Honor?"

She cleared her throat. "Actually, we didn't go shopping."

There was something in her tone that put me on alert.

I turned so I could face her completely, parting my legs and sliding so she was in between them. "What's going on?"

"I would have said something before. I just… I wanted to be sure."

She was starting to scare me. She looked a little scared herself. "Charlie, you can tell me anything." I tucked a strand of hair behind her hear.

"I'm pregnant," she said, the words bursting between her lips and being carried away by the wind.

It took a moment to register, for me to understand.

"You're pregnant?"

She glanced at me, a small smile playing on her lips. "We haven't exactly been careful."

Well, no, we hadn't. I pretty much wanted her anytime, anywhere, and she never turned me down.

Her hand went protectively to her belly, the belly that now held my child. "Tucker?" she asked, her voice a little unsure.

I gave a shout of joy and scooped her up, letting her tight ass fill my lap. My hand slid over hers, and I grinned. "You're giving me a baby." I couldn't keep the wonder out of my tone.

"Are you happy?" she asked. "I know it wasn't planned."

I grabbed her face and kissed the shit out of her until my chest screamed for air. "The best things in life are never planned."

She laughed.

"I can't think of anything I want more than my child growing inside you."

She smiled. It was a smile that rivaled the glittering ocean beneath the sun.

"Are you happy?" I asked, leaning my forehead against hers.

"So happy." Her eyes grew misty.

"Pregnancy hormones already?" I teased. "Guess I'm going to have to start carrying tissues in my pocket to dry your eyes."

She giggled. "I'm actually twelve weeks already."

I put my hand back against her belly once more. "You're a stealthy little one, aren't you, son?"

"Son?" she asked, lifting her brow.

"It's a boy," I said. I could feel it in my bones.

"I hope he's just like his daddy," she whispered.

I kissed her.

"Is it safe to come down?" A voice carried down from above.

I ripped my lips from the mother of my child and looked up to where Nathan and Honor were standing arm and arm, looking down at us.

"Get the cigars!" I yelled. "We're having a baby!"

Nathan's shout of joy filled the air.

Charlie laughed. She was absolutely glowing. "I love you so much."

"Not as much as I love you," I replied. I was getting damn good at saying pretty words.

"This life is so much better than the one I mapped out for myself," she said, resting her head against my shoulder.

I couldn't help but wrap my hand around her belly again. "Stick with me, babe. It's going to be one hell of a ride."

And it was.

THE END

ACKNOWLEDGEMENTS

This is the portion of the book where I dazzle you with my sparkling personality and witty wit. Okay, I doubt I have ever dazzled anyone with anything other than a flashlight. But seriously, usually in these here acknowledgments I don't go on for half an hour, listing the same people I always list, because ain't nobody got time for that.

Instead, I like to talk about what I was doing while I was in the process of writing this book.

Tricks was supposed to be out in January. Well, that was my plan… and you know what they say about the best laid plans.

No seriously, what do they say about that?

Anyway, I was pretty mentally drained from writing the first five books of the series in such a short amount of time, and then the holidays happened. And life happened.

Long story short, I got busy and I fell behind.

So when the calendar rolled over to 2014 and my kids went back to school, I rolled up my sleeves and got to work. I gotta tell you it was a struggle at first. I felt like I was walking through knee-high sludge (You ever see that bad B-rated movie from like forever ago called *The Blob*? That's what it felt like I was walking through. The Blob).

I worried that Tucker and Charlotte would suck. I worried that no one would like them. I worried I would torpedo my career with a craptastic book.

But then Tucker started talking to me. He started talking about his junk a whole lot. At first I was scandalized! I thought about changing all his colorful terms for his male anatomy because I was afraid people would be offended (and I was mildly embarrassed), but then I changed my mind. Besides the fact I found Tucker utterly amusing, I felt like changing everything he said to fit into a box I thought people would deem appropriate was wrong. He was saying those words in my head so why I shouldn't I write them? I always want to be as true to the characters as I can be.

So that being said, I hope you enjoy Tucker too. He is most definitely the most horny guy I've written to date. Ha-ha-ha-ha.

Charlotte was a little different than I imagined as well and I often worried people would lose respect for her because she sleeps with Tucker so quickly. I worried people would hate her for sleeping with Max's brother. But again, I went with the story the characters were whispering and hoped people would understand. But the more I wrote, the more I realized Charlotte was just human… She was like a lot of people in this world. On a certain path, doing what she thinks she has to be doing, and completely ignoring her innermost feelings and desires. I actually respect Charlotte a lot and I hope everyone sees at least some of what I tried to do with her character.

Tricks didn't really turn out the way I thought it would. I can't really tell you what I thought it would be… but it wasn't how it ended up. But I truly think it's better.

I really hope you all enjoy this one. It was such a pleasure to write. And I gotta give a big shout out to Tucker for helping bring my mojo back.

Like he says, he really is irresistible.

Before I close, I would like to acknowledge my family who didn't complain at all when I went into the cave and didn't come out for long periods of time. I'd also like to thank Percy Jackson for entertaining my children through his movies. Over and over again.

My daughter, Kaydence, wanted me to write in here that I am a candy stealer and I have a tendency to hide candy so they can't find it and I get it all to myself.

Hey, in my defense, if I don't hide it, I don't get any. A mom's gotta do what a mom's gotta do.

Also, to my editor at Gathering Leaves, Cassie McCown, thanks once again for always being there to clean up my mistakes. I couldn't do this without you. To Regina Wamba, who has some seriously HOT models that she lets me use on my covers, creating a total drool-worthy moment when you see my covers. To Sharon Kay, for formatting my stuff with such dedication and persistence. I consider myself lucky to have such a great team behind me. I truly couldn't do this without them.

And props to all you readers. You make what I do worth it. Thank you for helping me spread the word about my books and thank you for reading.

See you next book!

Turn the page for a sneak peek of,
TATTOO,
the next *Take It Off* novel,
coming March 2014!

TATTOO

Sneak Peek

Taylor

"This is 9-1-1. Please state your emergency."

The voice on the other end of the line was calm and cool, no indication at all that whoever they were would be bothered by the panic that surely waited on the other end of line.

On my end of the line.

But I didn't speak. I couldn't. I was scared, I was shaking… and I was afraid they would hear me.

"9-1-1, please state your emergency, the voice said again."

If I just sat here, if I just put the phone down where no one would see, could I be traced? Would the operator know to send help to this address? I was using my cell phone. Could a cell phone be traced like that?

My stomach churned because I honestly didn't know.

How stupid could I be? How could I have never taken the time to learn this? How could I be crouching here, under my counter, with sweat dampening my silk shirt and prayer whispering from my lips?

"I said down on the floor, now!" an angry voice demanded.

The cries and screams of people behind me echoed through my head. The sound bounced around in my brain, refusing to fade away and threatening to take away what little bit of grip I had on my sanity.

I couldn't just sit here.

I couldn't just watch my life flash before my eyes. I couldn't just let this happen.

I had to *do* something.

"I'm at Shaw Trust on Sunderland Avenue," I whispered. "There is a bank robbery in progress."

"Are you inside the bank, ma'am?" the dispatcher asked. I could hear her fingers flying over some keyboard and I prayed that meant she was sending help.

"Yes," I whispered, clutching the phone.

One of the robbers was yelling at Brandy, one of my fellow tellers, to open the safe, and she was crying loudly.

"How many intruders are in the bank?"

I wasn't sure. They charged inside in a flurry of furious movement and I ducked low, hiding myself behind my counter. "Too many," I breathed.

"I'm dispatching several units to the scene, ma'am," the operator informed me.

My stomach twisted painfully as the man continued to shout at Brandy. He was threatening her now and it seemed to make her more hysterical. Anger burned up through my esophagus. Anger at the robbers, anger at the woman on the other end of the phone. How could she be so calm? Did she not hear the commotion going on in the background? Did she not know that our lives were in danger?

A shot rang out and Brandy screamed. I peeked out to see plaster from the ceiling rain down over Brandy's head. She threw her arms up around her for protection, and the man with the gun—the man who shot into the ceiling—grabbed her by the back of her head and slammed her into the safe. "Open it!" he roared.

"Ma'am, were those shots fired?" the operator asked.

"Yes," I hissed, my voice shaky. "Please hurry."

I could hear the people from the lobby sobbing and my thoughts went immediately to the man just on the other side of my counter. I didn't know him, but the thought of him being hurt made my stomach hurt even more.

"What the hell is this?" someone snarled above me, and I quivered.

The phone was snatched away from my ear and I whimpered as a man in tattered jeans with a wide chest and a very lethal-looking gun in his hand snarled at me. He pressed the phone to his ear and I could hear the voice of the operator asking me if I was all right.

Yeah, *now* she was concerned.

With a loud roar, he threw the phone down onto the shiny tile floor and it broke apart, shattering instantly. The sound of scattering pieces was nearly as loud as the gunshot just moments before.

"We gotta snitch!" he yelled, reaching down. I pressed myself against the back of the counter until I felt the wood dig into the bones in my back. I slapped his hands away, but really it was useless. He outweighed me by at least fifty pounds. And he had a gun. My greatest weapon at the moment was my fingernails.

His hands were rough as he grabbed my wrist, twisting the flesh covering the bone and wrenching me out of the hiding spot. I cried out as he jerked my arm around my back, pulling so forcefully that it felt as if my shoulder was dislocated from its socket.

I didn't have time to really assess if it was or not because he jammed the barrel of the gun into my throat. I could feel my hammering pulse thump rapidly against the cold, hard metal of the weapon.

"You call the police, bitch?" he whispered in my ear. Little dots of spit sprayed the side of my head from his putrid mouth.

I didn't say anything because my answer would only make things worse.

The heavy footfalls of someone approaching from behind made me even more nervous, and I whispered another prayer in the back of my mind. We spun, and I was sandwiched between the guy threatening me with a gun and another thief staring at me with angry, dark eyes.

"You called the cops?" he said, like it was hard to believe.

"Last time I checked, robbing a bank and holding a gun on a person was a crime," I said, knowing I shouldn't, but not being able to keep the words in. I was scared, but I was also very angry.

He smacked me across the face. Hard.

His palm literally slammed into the side of my face, making my entire head fly sideways and right into the gun at my neck. The hard steel was unforgiving and it jammed into my flesh, making me cry out.

That was going to leave a mark.

"Hey," said a rough voice from off to the side. "I thought you were here for the money and not to hit women."

Part of me wanted to thank the man behind my counter for trying to defend me; the other part of me was horrified he would be punished.

Just as I feared, the man who slapped me leveled his gun at him. What was his name again? I tried to remember what it said on his ID when he showed it to me to make a withdrawal, but it was hard to think when half your face was stinging fiercely and the other half was being threatened with a bullet.

This was the worst day in the history of bad days.

"Hey! We came here for the cash!" another man behind us yelled.

I was shoved roughly forward. "Open the safe."

I wasn't going to open that safe.

I glanced at Brandy, who was huddled against the wall, crying. She didn't appear to be physically harmed and I breathed a sigh of relief.

"I said open it!" He yanked the gun away from my neck, but I couldn't enjoy the safety because he slapped his large, sweaty palm in between my shoulder blades and thrust me forward so forcefully that I slammed into the metal door of the safe and bounced back, falling onto my ass on the floor.

A thud echoed behind me as I was pulled to my feet. He placed the gun between my shoulder blades, holding it there and directing me until I was standing right in front of the large keypad that opens the safe.

"I don't know the combination," I lied.

"Then you better hope you're physic because you got exactly ten seconds to open that vault before I shoot you."

Well, if that wasn't motivation, I don't know what was.

On shaking knees, I stepped forward, pressing a number on the pad. Then I pressed a couple more. When I hit the release button, nothing happened. But I didn't expect it to. I just wanted it to look like I was trying to open it. I wasn't opening it.

"See," I said, my voice trembling. "I don't know."

I heard the distinct sound of sirens and screeching tires and gave a sigh of relief. The cops were here!

Of course, I barely had time to celebrate because the thieves did the one thing that had the power to make me reconsider opening that safe.

Brandy was snatched off the floor and a gun was pressed to her head.

"So help me God, if you don't open that shit right now, I will splatter her brains all over the wall."

Brandy started screaming and shaking. The man looked at me intently, like he couldn't hear her pleas. His eyes were empty inside, completely devoid of any kind of feeling. It's like he had some weird ability to shut off his emotions.

It made me wonder if he was a vampire.

I shook my head, telling myself that thinking about vampires was a sign I was cracking under pressure.

"I'll open it." I promised. Risking my life for the bank was one thing, but risking someone else's life for the bank was an entirely different entity.

After a few punches to the keypad, the lock clicked free and my stomach twisted. Someone twisted a hand in my hair from behind and pulled, practically ripping the strands from my scalp. I was tossed onto the floor, landing in a heap next to Brandy, who was still crying hysterically.

I backed up, wrapping an arm around her shoulder, as three men walked into the safe, the sounds of opening duffle bags like a stab to my heart.

"Thank you," Brandy whispered, and I turned my face up to look into her red-rimmed, bloodshot brown eyes.

"No money is worth anyone's life," I whispered back.

The voice of whom I assumed was a police officer boomed through the air, so loud that it came through the walls of the bank for all of us to hear. "The bank is surrounded. Release the hostages immediately," he demanded over an intercom.

Laughter floated from out of the vault and I figured that meant they didn't plan on letting us walk out of here. Silly me, I thought police presence would actually deter the robbers.

A large black duffle bag was tossed out of the vault, landing a few feet away. Crisp green bills were poking out of the top. Another one followed.

"Yo! Hurry up!" the guy guarding the door yelled to his friends, waving around a rather large gun. He turned toward the vault, disregarding the people cowering on the floor.

One of the women lying behind him jumped up and made a run for it, right toward the exit. The gunman turned and fired off a shot, catching her in the leg. She fell onto the floor with a high-pitched scream.

I watched in morbid fascination as a puddle of dark red formed around her.

People in the bank were sobbing openly now. Some of them were pleading for their lives.

I heard someone outside yell, "Shots fired!"

My eyes traveled around the room, seeking out the man whose name I couldn't remember. Our eyes locked and for one long second it was like we were the only two people in the room. He wasn't crying or begging for his life. He wasn't sweating or looking for a way to save his ass.

He was standing there, in the center of the room, calm and strong, like this situation wasn't that big of a deal. He made me feel better, more in control.

Another duffle flew out of the vault and one of the men stepped out. There had to be millions of dollars in those bags. Not only would it ruin this bank, the people who did business here, but my father as well.

My newfound strength made me brave.

I stepped in front of one of the bags, giving a level look to the men who intended to take it. "If you leave now, you might get away."

The man standing directly in front of me smirked and the smirk turned into a full-blown smile. I realized my mistake then.

I tried to entice them with freedom, with the thought of getting away unscathed. These men didn't care about that. If I had been thinking clearly, I would have realized that from the beginning. None of them were wearing ski masks or those plastic masks that looked like creepy clowns or animals. They weren't even trying to hide their faces.

Men who didn't hide their faces in a situation like this were either really desperate or really meticulous and had a fail-proof plan. They planned to be long gone before anyone could recognize their faces.

I wasn't going to stop them.

No one was.

The man standing in front of me raised his gun, pointing it right at me.

And then he pulled the trigger.

Cambria Hebert is the author of the young adult paranormal *Heven and Hell* series, the new adult *Death Escorts* series, and the new adult *Take it Off* series. She loves a caramel latte, hates math, and is afraid of chickens (yes, chickens). She went to college for a bachelor's degree, couldn't pick a major, and ended up with a degree in cosmetology. So rest assured her characters will always have good hair. She currently lives in North Carolina with her husband and children (both human and furry), where she is plotting her next book. You can find out more about Cambria and her work by visiting http://www.cambriahebert.com.

Tricks